Indulge Me

Also from J. Kenner

Stark Security
Shattered With You
Broken With You
Ruined With You

The Stark Saga:
Release Me
Claim Me
Complete Me
Anchor Me
Lost With Me
Damien

Stark Ever After:
Take Me
Have Me
Play My Game
Seduce Me
Unwrap Me
Deepest Kiss
Entice Me
Hold Me
Please Me
Indulge Me

**Stark International
Steele Trilogy:**
Say My Name
On My Knees
Under My Skin
Take My Dare (novella, includes bonus short story: Steal My Heart)

Stark World Standalone Stories:
Justify Me (part of the Lexi Blake Crossover Collection)

Jamie & Ryan Novellas:
Tame Me
Tempt Me

Indulge Me
A Stark Ever After Novella
By J. Kenner

1001 Dark Nights

EVIL EYE
CONCEPTS

Indulge Me
A Stark International Novella
By J. Kenner

Copyright 2019 Julie Kenner
ISBN: 978-1-948050-79-1

Published by Evil Eye Concepts, Incorporated

Sign up for the 1001 Dark Nights Newsletter
and be entered to win a Tiffany Key necklace.

There's a contest every month!

Go to www.1001DarkNights.com to subscribe.

**As a bonus, all subscribers can download
FIVE FREE exclusive books!**

One Thousand and One Dark Nights

Once upon a time, in the future…

*I was a student fascinated with stories and learning.
I studied philosophy, poetry, history, the occult, and
the art and science of love and magic. I had a vast
library at my father's home and collected thousands
of volumes of fantastic tales.*

*I learned all about ancient races and bygone
times. About myths and legends and dreams of all
people through the millennium. And the more I read
the stronger my imagination grew until I discovered
that I was able to travel into the stories... to actually
become part of them.*

*I wish I could say that I listened to my teacher
and respected my gift, as I ought to have. If I had, I
would not be telling you this tale now.
But I was foolhardy and confused, showing off
with bravery.*

*One afternoon, curious about the myth of the
Arabian Nights, I traveled back to ancient Persia to
see for myself if it was true that every day Shahryar
(Persian: شهريار, "king") married a new virgin, and then
sent yesterday's wife to be beheaded. It was written
and I had read, that by the time he met Scheherazade,
the vizier's daughter, he'd killed one thousand
women.*

Something went wrong with my efforts. I arrived in the midst of the story and somehow exchanged places with Scheherazade — a phenomena that had never occurred before and that still to this day, I cannot explain.

Now I am trapped in that ancient past. I have taken on Scheherazade's life and the only way I can protect myself and stay alive is to do what she did to protect herself and stay alive.

Every night the King calls for me and listens as I spin tales. And when the evening ends and dawn breaks, I stop at a point that leaves him breathless and yearning for more. And so the King spares my life for one more day, so that he might hear the rest of my dark tale.

As soon as I finish a story... I begin a new one... like the one that you, dear reader, have before you now.

Chapter One

Damien watched from the bungalow's back porch as his daughters chased the surf. The waves rolled in relentlessly, and the girls—giggling and happy—scampered forward and back with the joyful determination of children.

A few feet away, Nikki sat on a blanket sipping from a bottle of water, her eyes fixed on their kids. Her blond hair gleamed in the island sun, and her skin had turned a golden brown in the five days they'd been at the resort. She hugged her knees, and though he could only see her in profile, there was no missing the beatific smile on her lovely face.

The sight warmed him, and he felt his entire body relax. It had been almost three months since his family had been freed of the nightmare surrounding Anne's kidnapping. Though, of course, they'd never be truly free. He saw that reality reflected back at him every day when he looked in Nikki's eyes and glimpsed the shadows there. The remnants of pain, the residue of defeat. And, most of all, the lingering fear that clouded her face and poisoned her happiness.

In the days immediately following the ordeal, it had been Nikki who'd brought him back from his own grim descent into guilt and pain, and once he'd pulled himself together, he'd been so damn cocksure that the bond between them had once again beat back the horror that the world had thrust upon them.

And for a time, maybe it had.

But in the last week, he'd watched as dark shadows returned to his wife's eyes. He'd felt helpless, and that wasn't a sensation he endured easily. He'd needed to act. To do. To help. And so he'd brought her here as an escape against a world that had turned dark and dangerous. An isolated island world that he had built.

Conceived by Damien's sister-in-law, Sylvia, and designed by his brother, Jackson Steele, The Resort at Cortez was a high-end vacation property that had finally come to fruition via a route of scandal, vandalism, and even murder. It had shed that horrific past, though, and now it was a place of healing. A second home where, Damien hoped, Nikki could find both peace and escape.

Now he stood on the patio of their bungalow in the private owners' section of the island. Other than his wife and daughters, the beach was empty as far as he could see in both directions, and on this side of the island, there was no view of the California coastline. They were alone, just the four of them in this sun-swept world.

And that, he thought, was what Nikki had needed.

But it wasn't enough.

He closed his eyes, not wanting to hear the small voice in his head. The voice that knew that the calm and beauty of this island was only a Band-Aid against a much larger wound. A wound that, so far, Damien had been helpless to staunch.

Frustrated, he clutched the patio rail, wishing he had the strength to shatter the wood beneath his hands, because then maybe he could find the strength to help his wife. He wouldn't— *couldn't*—fail her. But, dammit, he still hadn't found the key that could lock away her pain.

Frustration warred with need, and he took a step toward the stairs, intending to go to her, but the sharp chirp of his phone stopped him.

That ringtone was the one assigned to Ryan Hunter, his closest friend and the Chief of Security for Stark International.

Technically, Ryan still held that title, but he'd recently delegated the day-to-day management of all Stark-related corporate security, thus freeing him up for his role as the head of the newly formed Stark Security Agency.

"How's Nikki?" Ryan asked without preamble.

"Good," Damien said automatically, then, "Why are you—"

"Jamie's worried about her, too." Jamie Archer—now Jamie Hunter—had been Nikki's best friend since before Damien knew either of them. Beautiful, brash, reckless, and outspoken, Jamie was like a force of nature. There was also no one he trusted more where Nikki was concerned.

"What's she said?" Damien asked.

"It was odd, actually. This morning she mentioned that Nikki had been doing so well, between time passing and you and counseling."

"But?"

"That's what was odd. Then she said *that damn car spoiled everything.*"

"What the hell does that mean?"

"That's what I asked, but Jamie said it was a BFF confidence, which I'd normally respect, but with Nikki and everything that happened, I decided to push."

Damien's chest tightened. He knew Ryan was referring to Nikki's cutting. She hadn't cut for years, not since before she and Damien got together. At least not until Anne's kidnapping. Then she'd taken a blade to her skin. Only once, and not deep. But she'd done it.

She'd worked with a counselor, publicly talked about it, and even started volunteering with troubled teens, but Damien still worried that the hated scalpel had opened not just her skin, but a door to the shadows that now seemed to haunt his wife.

"And? So what did Jamie say?"

"Nothing. I pressed, and I think she would have told me, but then Jeffery got sand in his eye—we were babysitting for Syl and Jackson at the playground this morning—and before I had the chance to ask what she meant, she and the kids were heading off to meet Syl. You'll probably see her before I do, but I can call and ask if you want."

"No, that's okay." Jamie was coming to the island that evening so that Nikki would have company over the next few days while Damien was in Paris on business. Sylvia and Jackson were already on site, along with their son and daughter. "I'll either ask her in the morning or find out from Nikki."

"Nik hasn't said anything to you?"

Damien frowned. "No. Maybe that means it's nothing at all."

"Maybe," Ryan said, but Damien could tell his friend didn't believe that any more than Damien did.

"While I appreciate your concern about my wife, I'm assuming that wasn't the primary purpose of this call?"

"I wanted to update you," Ryan said, his voice now firmly professional. "Denise has moved fully over to Stark Security, although I still can't get her to do field work. Even so, she's one hell of an asset in tech."

"Keep pushing," Damien said, thinking of the competent blonde with the sharp green eyes. When her husband had disappeared during a covert government mission, she'd left her own intelligence job for a position at Stark International. Damien understood her desire to avoid the field, hiding herself away behind a keyboard. But he'd also seen the dossier Ryan had put together, compiled through both legitimate and not-so-legitimate means. The woman had talent. Stark Security would take her any way it could have her, but Damien wanted her in the field where she could be the most use.

Created after Anne's kidnapping, Stark Security was the tangible manifestation of Damien's need to not only protect his family, but to help others in similar positions. To fight against those who oppressed the innocent, and fill the gap between what the authorities could do, and what needed to be done. It was Damien's passion project, and it was his current mission to populate it with the most talented people he could find.

"Don't worry. I'll keep on Denny. And Liam's in," Ryan added. "Not much of a surprise there. He made noises about retiring, but I never believed him."

"Liam Foster is an asset," Damien agreed. "Good work."

"Hey, you're the one with the relationship to Deliverance," Ryan pointed out, referring to the now-defunct vigilante group to which Liam had once belonged.

"And Quincy?" Damien asked, referring to another former Deliverance operative who had helped out with the investigation into Anne's kidnapping.

"He's still dragging his feet. But I think he's leaning toward signing on. That's the main reason I called. To tell you to give him a shout. Maybe even make a stop in London before you head on to Paris."

"I'll give him a call and see if he's available. He's still working for MI6, so he could be anywhere."

Ryan chuckled. "Maybe he's visiting Antonio in Paris."

"That would be convenient." Damien was primarily traveling to Paris for a series of meetings with the head of the development team at the French division of Stark Applied Technology. But while he was there, he intended to meet with Antonio Santos, another former member of Deliverance, and a man with the kind of skills, experience, and hard edges that would make him an asset at Stark Security.

"Daddy! Daddy!" Lara's high-pitched voice caught his attention and he looked up to see that Nikki had joined the girls in the surf. Now his four-year-old daughter jumped and clapped as Nikki held Anne, their two-year-old, under her arms, and was swinging her up and down so that Anne's little feet skimmed the waves as they rolled in.

"Come do me, Daddy!" Lara demanded. "Come do me!"

"In a minute, baby," Damien called back, basking in the wide smile that Nikki tossed his way. A smile that flashed as bright and pure as the sky above. A smile that made it seem as if she didn't have a care in the world.

Damien knew better.

"I'll call him now," Damien said, driven by the sudden urge to get Stark Security fully staffed. He wanted the SSA to be out there in the world, fighting anything that put a shadow on his wife's face and destroying the kind of evil that had stepped inside the perimeter of Damien's life and laid a hand on his child and her nanny.

Quincy answered on the first ring. "Radcliffe."

"It's Damien. Are you in London?"

"Malta, actually. Then I'm on to Prague, Milan, and Copenhagen." His voice was crisp, his British accent pronounced. "It's a bloody tour of Europe, and not one I signed on for."

Damien chuckled. "Considering the laundry list of locations, I take it this isn't a covert operation. Because if it is, I'm going to have to rethink our offer to bring you on at Stark Security."

"Stick with tennis and science, Mr. Stark. Comedy isn't your thing."

"A diplomatic tour? When will you be back in London?"

"I'm on the road for a month. It's a bloody nightmare. And, no, I'm not going through Paris, so meeting there isn't an option."

"Ryan mentioned my itinerary to you," Damien said. "To me, he mentioned that you're considering our offer."

"I am. I have been since we spoke in Malibu. It's a good offer, Stark. But I also told you I was thinking about retiring."

"And now you're thinking about staying in."

"True. But thinking and doing aren't the same thing. And if I stay in this business, I can't go on serving two masters." In what Damien assumed was a rare arrangement, Quincy had been an MI6 agent even while working with Deliverance. "I assume you know that, too," Quincy continued. "Or guessed it. And that you want to have a sit-down to push me over the line toward Stark Security and away from MI6."

"But it looks like I'll have to settle for this phone call."

Damien could almost hear the smile in Quincy's voice when he said, "I'm listening."

Damien drew in a breath, letting the sight of Nikki and the girls focus his thoughts. "I need to make this happen. Stark Security. I need it to be more than just another entity under the Stark umbrella. I need it to be formidable. Hell, I need it to be dangerous. I need it to be the line in the sand between the kind of world that should exist, and a world filled with monsters disguised as humans. I need it, Quincy, because I have to know that I'm making a difference. For my family. For the world. And that means I need good people. People who've seen a world where the monstrous has taken root and have vowed to do something about it." He drew a breath. "I think you're one of those people."

"Maybe I am. Maybe I've already done my share. More than my share."

"I don't doubt that you have." His eyes were fixed on Nikki, but his mind was remembering the moment he'd learned that Anne had been taken. The icy horror that had enveloped him, and the way the entire world had turned black, blotted out by rage and despair. "I don't doubt it," he repeated softly. "But I hope you'll do more."

He needed Quincy. Needed Ryan and Denise and Liam and Antonio all the rest. He needed them because he couldn't do it alone.

Couldn't wave his arm and make the world over the way he wanted.

Couldn't wipe away the dangers and destroy all the monsters.

Hell, he couldn't even wipe the fear from his wife's eyes.

But Stark Security? *That*, he could do.

And it was a damn good start.

Chapter Two

My arms are aching by the time I collapse to my knees, then fall on my back into the sand as I hug Anne to my chest, both of us laughing.

"More, Mommy! More swing! More swing!"

"You've worn me out," I say, reaching down for a handful of wet sand to dribble on her back. Her fine blond hair is in eight ponytails all over her head, courtesy of her older sister, and her nose is turning red despite the constant slathering of sunscreen.

She's wearing a yellow toddler two-piece decorated with pink fish, and she squeals when the Pacific-chilled sand touches her skin, then bursts into a fresh round of giggles before once again returning to her "More swing!" chorus.

"Why don't you go help Lara?" I suggest, glancing toward my oldest, who is currently focusing all of the engineering skills she's acquired in her four years on this earth to the problem of building a castle and moat.

"Mommmeee!" Lara scowls at me from under her black bangs, a few errant red strands of which catch the sun. "She'll mess it up."

"Wanna swing! More swing!"

"No more swing. And as for you," I add to Lara, "why don't

you give her a task? Like building an outer moat."

Her forehead crumples a bit, then she nods, as regal and self-assured as her father always is. "She can build the dinosaur pen."

"That sounds perfect," I say, working very hard not to laugh.

"Please!" Anne rocks on my torso, drawing my attention back to her. "Wanna swing!"

"Not happening, kid." I try to rise, but it's not easy getting up off of sand with twenty-six pounds of determined two-year-old straddling your rib cage.

I'm about to tell her that she's done me in and needs to get off when that problem is magically solved. She scampers up and scoots away, her little heel slamming into a possibly important internal organ. My *oof* is drowned out by her ear-splitting squeal of *Daddy!* It echoes across the beach as she races forward, moving fast out of my field of vision to disappear behind me.

I roll over so that I'm on my stomach, my elbows in the sand as I prop myself up in what probably looks like a poor attempt at the Cobra Pose. I stay that way, the sun warming my back and the cool froth of the surf tickling my legs while I watch Damien's long-legged stride as he approaches from the bungalow.

I sigh, not sure I could move if I wanted to. I'm too lost in the look of him, in the confidence of his movements, even for something as trivial as crossing a beach. There's never a time that I've seen him look awkward or out of place. And right now is no exception. He looks like he was born to this island with his tan skin, unbuttoned white shirt, and khaki shorts.

Damien Stark. One of the most powerful men in the world, and he belongs to me. My husband. My whole universe, really. The man who loves me and our daughters beyond anything in this world.

The man who knows my secrets. Most of them, anyway. I'm hoping that I've managed to hide this new sense of doom I can't seem to shake, the emotional shrapnel of a battle lost even though the war was won.

I've felt it for about a week now, brought on by a random

moment interrupting a beautiful day. It wasn't until we came here, to the island, that the dark clouds in my mind parted, letting sunshine back in.

The island.

My stomach twists with the realization that I haven't managed to hide my troubles at all. On the contrary. We're here because Damien saw. And because he's trying to help.

I drop my gaze, feeling exposed.

"Daddy! Daddy!" Lara joins the fray, and I lift my head again in time to see Damien scoop them both up, the effort revealing the strength in those arms.

I'm never guilty of forgetting that before my husband became a master of the universe, he was a star athlete. But sometimes I do forget what that means, and I'm reminded in moments like this. When he's working out in our gym, playing tennis on our court, or effortlessly lifting our kids.

"Put one girl in each arm and you could do flies," I suggest as I rise to my feet. "Is that what they're called?" I raise my arms to my sides, miming holding weights.

"If I'm going to do that, we'll need to feed this one more," he says, bouncing Anne, who has switched from giggles to big belly laughs. "Otherwise, I'll be uneven."

"Can't have that," I say as he deposits both kids back on the sand. "I'm fond of my symmetrical husband."

I've been walking toward him, and he toward me. Now we're just inches apart.

"Hello, Ms. Fairchild."

"Hello, Mr. Stark." I hear the breathiness in my voice and feel the reaction in my body. Years of marriage and two children, and he still takes my breath away and makes my body burn.

"Go on," he says, his eyes never leaving mine as he speaks to the girls. "I need to talk to Mommy."

"Talk or kiss?" Lara demands, and I watch as Damien tries very hard not to smile.

"Probably both," he says, eyeing our oldest sternly. "If that's okay with you."

Her mouth purses and her brow furrows as she considers the question. Then she nods solemnly. "It's okay, Daddy."

"Thank you, Lara." He points to the castle. "Off you go."

"*Probably* both?"

"Both," he says firmly as he moves closer, his palm cupping the back of my head, his fingers twining in my windblown hair. He tugs, not painfully, but demanding, and forces my face up. Then his mouth is on mine, his other arm around my waist as he kisses me long and deep.

As kisses go, we'd still warrant a G rating. But the sizzle that burns inside me? The sparks that zing between the two of us?

Well, that's got NC-17 written all over it.

"I like seeing you this way," he says as soon as our lips part.

"On a beach in a bikini?" I tease.

"Well, yes, actually, but that wasn't what I meant. I was thinking how free and happy you look here. Fearless," he adds, then cups my cheek, his eyes locking on to mine.

I conjure a smile. "This is home. At least as much as Malibu is. What's there to fear?" But I'm looking at his mouth as I speak, not his eyes, and I'm certain that my husband—a man who I should know misses nothing—sees that.

"Nikki, sweetheart. What's going on?"

He brushes my cheek and I realize that he's wiping away a tear.

"I don't know," I whisper.

"Something to do with a car?"

I almost smile. "Jamie is *so* in the doghouse now."

He grins. "No, she was talking to Ryan. Said something about a car, and then clammed up when he asked her what she meant, and she realized she'd blown a confidence. But she was worried about you, and—"

"Ryan told you," I finish, half-irritated and half-pleased. Because as much as I want my secrets, it feels nice knowing that my friends love me.

"The car?" he presses.

"It sounds so ridiculous," I begin. "It was last Saturday. I'd gone to a movie with Abby, remember?" Abby is my partner at Fairchild & Partners Development, and we'd decided to celebrate landing a new client by going out for a movie that afternoon.

He nods. "I remember. The girls and I played in the pool, then watched *Finding Nemo*."

"Right. Anyway, I came back down Mulholland." The famous road winds its way along the ridgeline of the Santa Monica mountains, and the views of both the San Fernando Valley and the west side are stunning. I've always loved navigating those hills and curves, the radio blaring and the windows open.

I always used to love it, anyway. Hopefully I will again.

Damien's voice is harsh as he says, "What happened?"

"Nothing," I say, taking his hand to calm the fury I see rising in his eyes. "Really, it turned out to be nothing. Which is why this—this *feeling* is so frustrating."

"All right. Tell me."

"I was driving, and it was a gorgeous day. I was listening to Tom Petty's *Freefalling* because, well, because it's the perfect song for that drive. I had it up loud, and the windows down, and I felt fabulous. The movie had been good. The air felt great. And I hadn't thought about the kidnapping in hours and hours."

I glance up at him, but he says nothing, so I draw a breath and continue.

"It must have come from a driveway or pulled out of a turnaround. I think I would have noticed if it had been behind me for any length of time."

"The car," he says, and I nod.

"It was red. Even after all these years with you, I didn't recognize the make. But it was sporty. And loud. That's what I noticed first. The roar of the engine as it came right up on my tail. Inches away," I tell him, hugging myself as I remember the way my heart started to pound.

"Son of a bitch." The muscles in his face are tight, and I can see the anger building behind his eyes.

"You know how curvy that road is. How narrow. And there aren't guard rails. I slowed down, and they got right up on my bumper. But I didn't want to go faster. Take those curves too fast, and—"

"I know."

"And then they went around me." I draw in a breath as I remember. "They passed on a curve. If the driver had shifted right and hit me from the side, I would have gone over. I tried to slow and fall back, but they did, too. And I was terrified that someone would come from the opposite direction, see them first, and move to my lane to get out of the way. There'd be no place for any of us to go except off the mountain."

I realize that he's taken my hand and smile up at him, relishing the comfort that this simple touch gives.

"There was a turnout coming up. I thought I should pull into it, but then I was afraid they would as well. And I couldn't actually dial my phone without risking losing control of the car, and voice commands weren't working. Probably because the signal is so crappy there. At any rate, I couldn't call 911 or you."

I can still taste the terror. The fear that I was either going over that mountain or the guys in that car were going to force me off the road and—well, I really didn't want to think about the *and*.

"What happened next?" His voice is hard, his words measured.

"They matched my speed. The passenger window was tinted. I only glanced over for a second. I needed to keep my eyes on the road. But then the window came down, right about the time we hit a straightaway. I noticed it out of the corner of my eye. And I glanced over and this kid was there in the passenger seat. Just your average kid, probably a senior in high school, maybe a freshman in college. I couldn't see the driver, but the guy in that passenger seat was guzzling beer. Maybe they both were. And then he put his fingertips to his lips, blew me a kiss, and the driver hit the gas. A few seconds later they were gone. It was just me and the mountain."

"Oh, baby." He folds me into his arms, his palm rubbing circles on my back as I cling to him, feeling stupid.

"I had to pull over," I whisper. "I had to sit in a goddamn turnout for fifteen minutes before I stopped shaking. They were kids. Just stupid kids out joyriding. And yet they scared me so much my skin still prickles from thinking about it."

"Rightfully so," he says. "If they'd lost control of the car. If they'd had a blowout, or you had. Or if another car had been coming toward you…"

He presses a hard kiss to my forehead, then moves his hands so that he's cupping my face. "This is not an irrational fear, sweetheart. And it's a good thing you don't have the license plate or else I swear to God, I'd go to those assholes right now and wring their necks." His eyes narrow. "Do you?"

"No. I thought about it, but they didn't have a front plate, and when they were beside me I couldn't see the rear one. By the time they shot away, I was too freaked to remember."

"Probably just as well. I don't have time right now to defend myself against a murder charge."

I actually smile at that. "Thank you. But it's not just them. I mean, yes, I was scared. But you're right. *That* fear is legitimate. It's the other, though…"

"The other?"

I nod, trying to find the words. "It's like I've been looking at the world through rose-colored glasses, and they stripped them away."

"Rose-colored glasses?" I hear the incredulity in his voice. "Our daughter was kidnapped. There's nothing rosy about that."

"We got her back," I whisper, tears pricking my eyes as I point toward Anne. "And she doesn't even remember a moment of it." I squeeze his hands. "You and I were broken when we met, Damien. Sliced into bits by the hell of our childhoods. Me, literally," I add, and am gratified by his ironic grin.

I squeeze his hands tighter. "All of the crap we went through before we got married—we survived. And then later, too. The miscarriage. The kidnapping. We've survived them all. We survived the dark together."

"Yes," he says, his brow furrowed in confusion. "Yes, we have."

"I've relied on that. I've been nursing the illusion that you and I live in some magic bubble where everything will turn out for the best. But don't you get it? Damien, the bubble's burst. And even though we survived, I can't help but be afraid of what's still hiding out there in the dark."

Chapter Three

I've been dreading this conversation, but now that we're having it, I can't help but feel relieved. Because I don't want to keep my wounds from Damien. Not when he's the one who has always helped me heal.

I used to joke that Damien could remake the world to his will with nothing more than a sweep of his arm, and if that wasn't enough, his checkbook could take over, and he'd remake it with a swipe of his pen. An exaggeration, of course. A joke, even.

And yet some small part of me believed it to be true.

No. Some part of me *knew* that it was true. Maybe not as to the whole world, but as to us. Him. Me. The girls. Our friends. Inside the bubble we lived in, Damien had that power. Even when the outside world would squeeze in through a pinhole, somehow Damien would shoot them down and shoo them away.

Anne's kidnapping was a huge breach in that bubble. But even then, Damien's command and determination pulled us through, and we got our daughter back.

We also got pain and fear and death and betrayal. And defeat, I add, thinking of the newest scar to mar my inner thigh.

Even then, it took some crazy teens on a winding road for me to finally understand just how dangerous the monsters in the dark can be.

I love Damien. More important, I trust him.

But I've finally faced the realization that he can't truly keep me or the girls safe any more than he could put that bubble back over our lives.

That's the truth. That's reality. And yet thinking it feels disloyal.

He's watching me tenderly, studying my face. "Tell me," he demands, and though it's difficult, I lead him through the twisting path of my thoughts.

"It's never bad when illusions are shattered," he says when I finish. "Facing reality is the truest form of courage there is. But that doesn't mean you have to give in to it. Instead, you acknowledge it. You look it in the eye. And in that moment, you know that you're strong enough to withstand anything. *You*, Nikki."

"Am I?" I know he believes it. He's always seen a wellspring of strength in me that even the fact that I took a blade to my own flesh couldn't squelch.

And the irony? He's right. I *am* strong. I'm even stronger with him at my side.

But I'm also afraid.

I think of the terror that burned through my blood on that dangerous mountain road. The similar pang I feel every time my girls leave my sight now, because I've seen the truth. I know that anything could happen to them. Anything at all. And not even a man like Damien Stark can ensure their safety.

I meet his eyes. "Can you honestly tell me that your heart doesn't tighten every moment they are out of your sight?"

"Our girls? Of course it does. Every moment you're away from me, too. But goddammit, I won't cower forever just because horror came knocking. And I won't let you, either."

I almost laugh, but I hold it back. I know this conversation is hard for him. Damien is a man who needs to be in control. But how can he control something uncontrollable, like an emotion?

Like fear?

"You're an incredible man, Damien Stark. The best man I've ever known. But you can't clear the path for me or for anyone. Not yourself. Not Anne or Lara."

"Nikki—"

"No. I'm not finished. This isn't about the car, not really. That was just a catalyst. Something that forced me to face a bigger reality. Before the kidnapping, I knew that bad things could happen. Now I know that bad things *do* happen. Monsters used to be the things of fairy tales. But they're real, Damien. We've seen them. And they're everywhere."

He gently pushes a strand of hair off my face. "That's why I'm building Stark Security. To fight for you. To fight for the whole world. And that's why I'm pulling in good people to help with the fight."

"I know that. And I think you're amazing. But I still can't—"

"Yes," he says, cupping my chin in his hand. "You can."

* * * *

Of course he takes control in that Damien way he has, and soon enough, we've helped the girls finish the castle and the dinosaur pen. We've packed up all the plastic rakes and shovels, gathered the mesh bags full of shells, and double-checked that no one's favorite toy has washed out to sea.

Damien drags the blanket away so that he can shake it out downwind from tender little eyes, and I plop empty juice boxes back into the small, soft-sided cooler I brought with us.

All things considered, you'd think we trekked across the island instead of down the boardwalk and across the sand.

Now we all head back to where the weathered boardwalk traverses the dunes, leading up to the owners' section of the resort. Our bungalow sits on two lots, and Jackson and Syl's occupies the two opposite lots immediately across the boardwalk from us. That's where we go now, as Damien has announced to the girls—and to me—that it's time for them to visit their cousins.

The girls have been coming here all their lives—or, more accurately, Anne has. Since we adopted Lara, she's been coming all of her life with us. Either way, they both know their way around, and they scamper ahead.

"Any particular reason you're getting rid of the kids for the afternoon, Mr. Stark?"

"Yes," he says, turning to look at me just long enough to flash the kind of smile I've seen him use when Stark International acquires the assets of a company it intends to completely reorganize.

I drag my teeth over my lower lip as I wonder what, exactly, he has in mind for me.

We find Jackson on his back porch, a stack of architecture magazines on the table beside him. He's paging through them, ripping out articles and photos that interest him and tucking them into a folder, then discarding the magazines' remains.

He looks up as we approach and smiles. Damien's half-brother, Jackson, shares Damien's dark hair and classic good looks. But whereas Damien's eyes have a dark intensity, Jackson's are an icy blue. "Did we screw up the time? Syl said you weren't dropping the girls off until tomorrow morning. She just took the kids to the ice cream parlor."

Anne's already squatting on the floor, her little hands reaching for the pile of magazine discards. Beside her, Lara grabs her crotch and announces that she needs to go potty.

"You know where it is," Jackson says. "Wash your hands."

"Okay, Uncle Jackson," Lara says at the same time Damien tells her to take Anne. I expect an argument, but to my surprise Lara takes her little sister's hand and leads her into the bungalow.

"I was hoping we could beg a babysitting favor," Damien tells Jackson. "I have plans for my wife tonight, and as much as I love my children, they don't fit my itinerary."

"Oh?" I tease. "What kind of plans are those?"

Damien looks at me, his expression reflecting a hint of surprise. "I assumed you knew. I plan on fucking you senseless."

"Damien!" Heat rises to my cheeks. I'd expected the plan. I didn't expect that he'd announce it in front of Jackson.

Jackson looks about to die with laughter. "You tossed a challenge in his lap," Jackson says to me, with a sideways nod to Damien. "Come on, Nik. You should know better than that by now."

My blush remains, but I have to laugh, too. "I should," I agree. "I really should."

We linger awhile, accepting sweet hugs and sloppy kisses from our girls before heading across the boardwalk to our bungalow. As soon as we're inside, I wrap my arms around Damien's waist and press close. He's already hard, and I'm already wet, and as far as I'm concerned, that's a very good thing.

"I think you mentioned something about fucking me senseless."

For a moment, he says nothing. Then he says, "Take off your clothes."

I do, my body hyperaware of the brush of air over my heated skin. I stand obediently, curious about the edge to his voice and wondering what he has in store for us tonight.

"Do you remember what I said at the beach?"

"I—" I frown, trying to recall.

"I said that I won't cower to fear. And I won't let you, either."

I nod, remembering. But I'm still confused. "So, you—"

"You'll do what I say, Nikki. Without question. Without argument."

I open my mouth, but I'm not sure if I'm intending to agree, argue, or ask a question. I see Damien smile, as if he understands my confusion.

"You're wondering why," he says, and I nod. "Two reasons. First, because it makes me hard when you submit to me. But it's the second reason that's the most important. Because I'm going to push your limits, wife of mine. I'm going to take you outside of your comfort zone. And you're going to do what I say, aren't you? Because I ordered you to."

"Yes." My voice is breathy, heavy with anticipation. "Yes, sir," I amend as he cocks a brow.

"And once I've pushed you to your limit over and over and over again, I'm going to demand one more thing of you. I'm going to order you not to be afraid. And what will you do then?"

My voice catches in my throat as I answer. "I don't know."

"You'll obey," he says simply. He closes the distance between us, then brushes his thumb over my lower lip. "Then you won't be afraid anymore."

"I don't think that's true," I whisper.

"Then we'll make it true. Because you *are* strong, baby. Strong enough to face your fear. Strong enough to survive. And do you know why?"

I shake my head.

"Because you know that no matter what, you will always—always—have my strength to lift you up."

A lump fills my throat, and though I don't even plan to say it, I find myself voicing my biggest fear, the one that is the motor for all the others. The one I don't like to admit, even to myself. "What if my biggest fear is losing you?"

"Oh, baby…"

He reaches for me, his fingertips grazing my collarbone, then down to caress the swell of my breast before he lifts his fingers from my body and gently cups my face. "Don't you know that could never happen?"

"I know you'd never leave me," I tell him, but I can't bring myself to speak the true horror. As if saying the words would be a challenge to the gods.

Damien, of course, understands me. "No," he says with a gentle smile. "Not even that. You will always, *always*, have my strength. Because while death might keep me from your side, it can't keep me out of your heart. Do you know why?"

I shake my head, overwhelmed by his words. By his love. And by what I understand he is trying to give to me.

"Because you've always been strong, baby. Strong and fearless. I'm just a lens that helps you magnify it. But if you had to, you could stand alone."

"Damien…"

"As long as I'm on this earth, you'll never have to."

I open my mouth to speak, but he shakes his head firmly. "No. Time to get on your knees, baby."

I don't hesitate. That's the game, after all, even though tonight feels like so much more than a game.

"There'll be no more talking," he orders once I'm on the ground, my ass resting on my heels. "Not a word unless I ask you a direct question. Do you understand?"

I nod, and earn a smile for my obedience.

"The only thing those lips are for tonight is my pleasure. Kissing me. Sucking my cock. Are we clear?"

Yes, I think as I move my head in a nod. *Oh, God, yes.* My entire body is tight with an anticipation that is almost too much to bear, especially when he walks toward me, his fingers nimbly unbuttoning his shorts.

He stops just inches from me, then reaches down to stroke my hair. "Show me how well you can use that beautiful mouth," he demands. "Make me come, Nikki. And when I do, I want you to swallow every drop."

Chapter Four

His cock might be hard, but right then Damien felt pretty damn impotent. He wanted to see her fearless, but at the same time he wanted her to know that fear wasn't a weakness, just one more thing to conquer.

Still, even with his famous powers of concentration, he couldn't think about that now. Not when her wide, kissable mouth surrounded his cock. When her tongue was doing something magical, and her fingers at the base were bringing the show home.

He reached out for the back of the sofa, steadying himself as a delicious pressure built inside him. Watching the movement of her head as she took him in. Letting a profound sense of awe overtake him from the simple knowledge that this incredible woman was his wife.

His.

And, goddammit, he took care of what was his.

"Enough," he said, the word more of a growl than he'd intended simply because of the rawness of the emotions that coursed through him.

She was on her knees, looking up at him, playing their game, surrendering to him because she trusted him. Not just to help her overcome her fears, but because she simply *did*. She trusted him. Forever. And in all things. And if that didn't fucking humble him...

How did he deserve such a woman? Honestly, sometimes it baffled him. He'd meant what he said about her being strong and determined. She'd made her own life, after all, coming to LA against all odds, with a plan and a fierce determination to succeed.

She'd had so much shit thrown at her over the years, too much of it because she'd fallen in love with him, and that had made her fodder for both the paparazzi and his enemies.

She was exceptional, and it wasn't fear he should be seeing in her eyes but determination.

Determination.

The word bounced in his head, teasing out a thought, maybe even a solution.

"In the bedroom," he ordered. "On your stomach, arms and legs spread."

She nodded, whispered, "Yes, sir," and hurried away.

He took his time following her, stopping first by the locked trunk in which they kept the kind of toys the kids really didn't need to see.

He opened the padlock and pulled out a few favorites, thinking that they'd do very nicely. He put them in a black velvet bag, then moved to the bedroom, pausing for just a moment to enjoy the view. His wife, gorgeous and naked and ready for him. Her skin glowing in the lamplight of the curtained room.

His body tightened all over again at the thought of taking her like that, right now.

With long strides, he moved into the room, pleased when she didn't turn to look despite the way her body stiffened. He knew she wanted to watch him, wanted to speak. And yet she stayed quiet, willing to submit because he'd told her to.

They called it their game, but it was as real as it got. The game represented the connection between them. The trust. The love. So much more, in fact, that he had to take another moment to simply revel in the power that was *them.*

He saw her squirm, and he chuckled. "Am I torturing you, Ms. Fairchild?"

"Yes," she whispered. "But it's the kind of torture I like."

He moved closer, running his hand over the swell of her ass. "Good. So do I."

He put the bag on the pillow where she could easily see it, then pulled out a flail. "Should I whip that sweet ass, then soothe it with kisses?"

"Yes, sir. Yes, please." He heard the breathy arousal that colored her voice, and it made his blood burn with need. But not now. Not yet.

Instead, he pulled out a blindfold and watched the quickening pulse in her neck as he gently placed it over her eyes, tightening the strap on the back of her head, then trailing his fingers over her hair, her neck, then down her back until he reached her rear. With one finger, he explored further still, slipping between her cheeks until his finger teased the tight muscles of her ass.

She drew in a breath, and he whispered and increased the pressure. "Should I plug you? Fuck you here?" He moved away long enough to pull out a glass butt plug. "Open your mouth," he demanded, then slipped it between her lips, wetting the glass before pressing the tip where his finger had been. Not entering her, but giving her the promise of that pleasure.

"Tell me you'd like this," he said as her breathing changed, her little moans and sighs making his cock throb painfully.

"Yes," she said, and he slid his hand down to palm her sex, finding her wet and ready.

"Yes," he acknowledged with a grin. "You would. But not now, baby."

"I—" she began, then stopped, obviously fearing she'd be breaking the rules.

He pulled out a coil of black bondage ropes, then wrapped

one end loosely around her wrist so that she'd recognize this new delight despite the blindfold. "Perhaps I should tie you to the bed. Take away your power to respond, make you unable to move to dilute any pleasure I choose to give you. Would that excite you? Flip you onto your back and stretch your arms tight above your head. Your knees wide so that there's no hiding how much you want it. Your ankles bound."

She whimpered but said nothing, just drew in a sharp, needy breath when his fingers slid inside her. She was so wet, so ready, and his cock was so damn hard. This was punishing them both, but what sweet punishment it was. "You want this," he murmured, thrusting harder as her hips moved involuntarily, her body craving to be filled.

"Yes, sir."

"Why?"

"Because…because I like the way it makes me feel."

"In that case, maybe I should just find some random man in the bar to come wield a flail. Would that make you wet?"

Her body went tight with distaste. "No, sir."

"No? The pain centers you, doesn't it? Pleases you? Arouses you? Why is it that you give the flail to me and not him, this imaginary man in the bar?"

"Because I love you, and I want you." Her words were firm, and he knew without a doubt they were true.

"And? You have to tell me the rest of it. The core of it."

Her breath was shaky. "Because I know it pleases you, too. Arouses you to control me, to take command of my pleasure."

"It does. And that is a lot to hand over to me. Why bestow such a precious gift on me? Why give me all that power?"

"Because I trust you." The words were simple, almost as if she was mentally saying, *duh*. But it was important that she say it. That she believe and truly feel it. Because that was the core of what he needed her to understand.

He lowered his voice, changing his tone. Leaving behind the seduction, but keeping the firmness. The hint of command and control. "Do you trust the universe, Nikki?"

Her brow furrowed, and she turned her head, as if she was trying to see him despite the blindfold. "No," she whispered. "Not anymore."

He moved around the bed, running his finger lightly over her skin as he bent over, his lips brushing her ear as he whispered, "Then don't give it your power."

"I—I don't understand what you mean."

"You will." He allowed himself a grin, thinking how much he was going to enjoy the days to come. "Tomorrow, school begins."

Chapter Five

I'm humming as I work in the kitchen, alternating between flipping eggs and peeking through the giant window to watch the gulls playing in the distant surf. It's just past eight, and the sand sparkles in the sunlight.

"You're in a good mood," Damien says as he comes in from the patio. He's in running shorts and a navy blue T-shirt, and looks unfairly yummy for someone who rolled out of bed and went for a jog. After so many years of marriage, though, I've come to terms with the inequity of it all. He awakes with all the vim, vigor, and sex appeal of a Roman god, while I get up looking like I pulled two shifts at an all-night diner.

But when you get right down to it, I got the better end of the deal. Or, at least, I got the better view.

"Not a good mood," I tell him, sliding the eggs onto plates before sliding myself into his arms. "A fabulous mood. After last night, how could I help but be?"

"I'll take that as a compliment." He reaches around me and snags a piece of bacon off the serving tray, dodging my quick slap to his hand.

"Good, because that's how I meant it. Although I may take it back if you're going to overstep your bounds by stealing bacon."

"Consider it an advance against future bacon to come." His gaze shifts up toward the large clock mounted on the wall, and I watch as his mouth curves into a frown. "No time for a walk on the beach with my wife."

"No, but you could walk with me to get the kids." I add bacon to his plate and slide it onto the breakfast bar, along with a fork, half an avocado, and a slice of buttered toast. "I figured I'd watch all four kids today in payment for Syl and Jackson giving us last night."

"I'd take you up on that," he says, moving around the island to sit on a stool, "except—"

"You have plenty of time to run with me to get the kids and still get a shower in," I assure him as I fix my own plate. He has a chopper coming in forty minutes to ferry him to the Santa Monica airport where Grayson's waiting to take Damien to Paris.

"Except..." he continues, drawing out the word, "neither one of us needs to go get the girls. Jackson texted earlier that they all went down to the snorkel pond." One of the features of the island is a natural lagoon that is protected by a rocky barrier the government built back when the island was used for military training. The so-called pond doesn't get any deeper than four feet and attracts quite a bit of sea life, making it a favorite place for little kids to splash in their floaties and masks.

He turns his attention to his breakfast as I try to process his words. "Not that I don't want the kids spending time with their aunt, uncle, and cousins, but why on earth didn't they wait for me?"

"Probably because you won't be joining them." He stabs a chunk of avocado. "You're coming with me to Paris."

"I—what? No, I'm not. We talked about this a dozen times. Abby and I are going to San Diego the day after tomorrow to meet a potential client, and you said you'd be so busy dealing with those prototypes that it was all you could do to squeeze in the meeting with Antonio."

"That was before." There's a firmness in his voice that I

recognize. His corporate warrior voice.

I cross my arms. "Before what?"

"Before I decided that we'd make it work."

"*You* decided?"

He's just taken the last bite of his breakfast, so his acknowledgement is a silent nod.

"Well, you can undecide. I'm not packed, and I'm not going to leave Abby in a lurch."

"Abby can handle it. You made her your partner for a reason. And I already talked to her. You don't even need to pack. Anything you need, we can get in Paris."

"Damien, I'm not—"

"Are you arguing with me? Because it sounds like you're arguing with me." His voice is still firm. No nonsense. But this time it's not a corporate warrior tone. It's much more personal than that. It's low and sensual and full of the promise of pleasure...or the threat of pain.

You will do what I say. Without question. Always.

It's the voice from last night, and I feel my body responding. My sex clenches in anticipation. My nipples tighten with arousal. I'm like Pavlov's fucking dog, and I shake my head, more in denial of my own traitorous body than in argument. But of course Damien doesn't know that.

"Yes," he says, striding around the island, his bare feet not detracting in the least from his commanding appearance. He twirls a strand of my hair around his finger. "What did we talk about last night? Or do I need to turn you over my knee to help you remember?"

Once again, my body responds to his words. It's as if I'm a desiccated sponge and every forceful word is a drop of water bringing me back to life.

Honestly, I'm tempted to push back just for the pleasure of his punishment.

And, yes, I know that all of this is part of his plan to help me chase away my lingering fears, and I'm still dubious that it will work. Right now, though, I don't care about plans or fears. All I care about is desire. Because right now, I can't deny my body's reaction. And massive fail or not, I'm certain I'm going to enjoy this experiment.

"All right," I say with a decisive nod. "But we should say goodbye to the girls."

He meets my eyes. "No."

I suck a breath in through my nose, hating the thought of not seeing them. Afraid that if I don't, fate will conspire against me, and I might never see them again. "Yes," I counter. "We can stop by the pond on the way to the helipad. I can't just leave. I haven't been away from them since the kidnapping."

He steps forward and takes my hands. "Sweetheart, I know."

Chapter Six

Since I hadn't intended to go to Paris, my wardrobe is entirely too casual. Loose cotton dresses, baggy shorts, flip-flops. In the past, I kept a nice dress or two for when we visited one of the resort's featured restaurants. But I'd recently taken them back to Malibu, intending to trade them out. Naturally, I haven't gotten around to that yet.

I settle on twill pants and a plain white T-shirt with cute sandals, which should be comfortable on the plane. Apparently we're going shopping when we get there. I'll restock my closet Parisian-style.

I give Damien a shout from the bathroom to let him know I'm almost ready, then pause in front of the mirror to check my makeup and run a brush through my hair.

I'm debating a ponytail when he walks in. He stops in the doorway, looks me up and down, then frowns.

"What?" I ask.

"I thought you said you were ready."

I study his face, confused, but he looks perfectly serious. "I—um, I figured this would be fine for traveling. What's the problem?"

"It's my fault," he says, as if he's just remembered

something. "I neglected to set out your outfit." He moves through the large bathroom to the equally large closet. When he returns, he's holding my trench coat.

It's neither cold nor rainy, and I'm still ridiculously confused.

"This," he says. "Wear this."

I start to point out that there's no need, when I realize what he means. He wants me to wear the coat. Only the coat.

I open my mouth to protest, then see the subtle shake of his head even as I hear the echo of his earlier words. *You'll do what I say, Nikki. Without question. Without argument.*

That's the game, after all.

So I shrug casually, as if this is nothing, then pull off my shirt. I toss it negligently across the padded stool in front of my dressing table. I follow with my bra, then my sandals, then pull my pants and underwear off together.

I walk slowly to him, enjoying his reaction, as well as the way his obvious desire lights a spark inside me. I take the coat with a smirk, then put it on. The silk lining glides smoothly over my skin, the sensation all the more erotic since this garment isn't meant to be worn next to bare flesh. I button the coat, but with only four buttons it gapes a bit more than I'd like. I cinch the sash firmly around my waist and feel slightly less exposed. Very slightly.

Then I stand in front of my husband, my arms to my sides, as if offering myself up for auction.

"Good," he says. "And you can wear the sandals."

"Thank you, sir."

"You'll stay this way all the way to Paris."

His words freeze me. I don't know what I'd been thinking—that this was a game to be played before we left the island?—but what he's suggesting had never even entered my mind.

"Damien, no—"

"Don't argue," he says, then glances at his watch. "There's no time to punish you now…"

"But—" I cut myself off. "Sir, may I speak freely?"

"You may."

"We'll be traveling almost a full day. The chopper to the Santa Monica airport. Refueling on the East Coast. All the way over the Atlantic."

"You're afraid someone will realize. Worse, that they'll see."

"Well, yes."

"All right," he says, and I sag with relief. "Embrace that fear."

I freeze. "What—"

"Without question. Without argument." He turns to head out of the bathroom, pausing to look back at me. "Get your purse. We need to get to the helipad. And Nikki," he adds, with just the hint of a smile, "while we're traveling—while you're afraid of what people might think or see—I want you to remember that seeing you face your fears pleases me."

I meet his eyes, roll my shoulders back, and nod.

* * * *

I've not flown much in the chopper, and after going from the island back to the mainland, I can unequivocally state that I prefer traveling with wings, not blades. The noise was intense, but not as much as the vibration. And while the sensation of helicopter motion combined with my hyper-aroused state was rather scintillating, there was no way to enjoy the sensations. Not with the pilot sitting just a few feet away from me and Damien.

The real downside, though, became evident when we boarded the Bombardier, the jet Damien uses primarily for intercontinental travel. I was drunk on sexual anticipation, my body hyper-aware of everything. And yet I had to board that plane, chat with Grayson, and then catch up with Katie, who's been the primary attendant with the Stark fleet for as long as I've known Damien.

"They know," I whisper to Damien now that we're buckled in for take-off, each with a glass of wine.

"They might," he says. "But they'll never be certain."

I grin at him, amused. The man has a point.

"I want to call the kids as soon as we're in the air."

"No," he says.

"Excuse me?"

"Are you afraid something's happened to them?"

"No," I say, because even though that was my reason for calling—to make sure all is well—I also know that it must be. Sylvia or Jackson would have called immediately if anything had happened, and if they contacted Damien, he would have told me. Even while playing this game, he wouldn't withhold information about our babies.

"I just—I hate leaving without saying goodbye."

"I know," he says gently. "I wouldn't whisk their mommy away with no word. I went by the pond on my run this morning and told them that Daddy's taking Mommy on a secret trip, gave them both kisses from you, and told them they had to help keep the secret."

I relax. I should have known Damien would anticipate my worries.

Take-off is uneventful, and as soon as Grayson's voice comes over the loudspeaker to let us know we've reached cruising altitude, I unbuckle and stand, my hand held out to Damien.

His brows raise. "Going somewhere?"

"The state room?" I mean it as a statement, but it comes out as a question.

"Maybe later," he says. "Right now, I think you should sit down." He nods at the adjustable couch that lines the copilot side of the jet. Each of the four segments extend, pulling out into four narrow beds divided by hidden arm rests that convert to bed rails, or into one full size bed if the rails are retracted.

In other words, it's large enough to comfortably do anything Damien has in mind.

Without thinking, I take a step backward. Damien's brows

rise, and I freeze. "Objections, Ms. Fairchild?"

I lick my lips, thinking. I know that Katie won't come in. There's a door between the passenger area and the galley where the crew stays. Still, it's a lot like having sex in the den while the kids are playing in their room.

I sigh and start to sit. Damien takes my elbow to prevent it. "It's warm in here. I don't think you need the coat."

My heart pounds, and I shake my head without thinking.

"Yes," he says. That's all he says.

I take off the coat, ignoring his tiny smile of triumph, and toss it onto one of the two armchairs on the opposite side of the cabin.

"Sit." Damien nods at one of the two middle seats, and I comply, feeling nervous and uncomfortable and, yes, aroused.

"You're so beautiful," he says, and there's no missing the desire in his voice. It both flatters and calms me. "Arms on the armrests, and spread your legs."

That extra bit of exposure adds to my nervousness, but I've already crossed the magic line, and I comply without hesitation.

He kneels in front of me, his hands on my knees. I close my eyes in anticipation of his mouth on my sex, then open them again in surprise when I feel the straps go around my right wrist. He's using Velcro bands to restrain me. And once he's done with my arms, he bends lower and secures my legs in place.

"Damien…" I can hear both nerves and arousal in my voice, and from the way he's smiling, I'm sure he can, too.

I wait, certain he'll tell me again to close my eyes. Certain he's going to go down on me or tease me with a vibrator or find some other way to fill me with a pleasure so potent I'll want to squirm away from it, and absolutely won't be able to. Honestly, I can't wait.

He walks away, then sits in one of the arm chairs.

I gape as he pulls out a leather file bag, then takes out a sheath I recognize as the technical specs for the prototype that is the focus of his upcoming meetings. When he leans back and starts reading, I scowl, realizing that I'm not getting anything I want. Not yet, anyway.

"You're enjoying this," I accuse.

He doesn't even look up from the papers. "Of course I am. That's the point."

I let out a resigned breath, and he puts the papers in his lap, giving me his full attention. "Do you remember our honeymoon in Paris?"

"Oh," I say innocently. "Did we go to Paris?"

He raises a brow.

"Yes, sir," I say. "Of course I remember it."

"And the club? À la Lune?"

"God, yes." My body reacts merely from the mention of the private sex club located in the Quartier Pigalle.

Early in our relationship, I'd dragged Damien into a dark, secluded alley, so desperate for him, I would have happily let him fuck me against the brick wall. He'd told me he didn't do public sex, and that has never changed. Not literally. But he's taken me in dressing rooms and limos—oh, God, the limos. He's made me come in restaurants, his fingers hidden beneath tablecloths, and fucked me in front of hotel windows. He's fingered me in dance clubs and made me touch myself in the passenger seat of convertibles.

At the club in Paris, we took things up a notch. We weren't public—on the contrary, we were well-hidden in a curtained alcove and still dressed. More or less. But we had a view of the couples and threesomes in the public area, all stroking and teasing like a cornucopia of sex. Except for porn, I'd never watched other people having sex, and I'd been surprised by how turned on the sight made me. Especially with Damien's hands on my breasts and his voice in my ear. And when he fucked me from behind while we both watched in the dark, I thought my body would rip apart from the pleasure.

"Do you remember why I took you there?"

"You said you didn't want us to ever feel too settled. Too

domestic." I glance down at my naked body, spread wide and tied down in an airplane seat. "I'm thinking domesticity isn't really an issue for us."

A laugh bursts from him. "God I love you."

"Ditto," I say happily. "But why are you asking?"

"We're going back. Tonight, after dinner."

"Oh." I draw in a breath, feeling my nipples tighten, my sex clench. Damien lifts a brow, and though he says nothing, I know he's well aware of my reaction. "And now?" I hear the anticipation in my voice, the longing for his touch.

He holds up the papers. "I have to prep for my meetings."

"Oh." I swallow. "You're really leaving me like this?"

"Mmm." He's already absorbed in the specs.

I watch him for a few moments, wondering if he's really focusing on work, but he must be because he never once looks at me. Instead, he makes a constant series of notes in the margins, flips pages back and forth as if cross-checking facts, and nods to himself.

Well, fuck.

I end up dozing, closing my eyes and letting the vibrations of the plane against my bare ass entice me into erotic dreams. Dreams that dissolve into reality when I wake up and find Damien on the ground in front of me, his hands under my ass and his tongue teasing my clit.

I arch back as much as I can, trying to scoot my hips forward, desperate to latch on to the rising excitement. Wanting it to pull me right over the edge and out to the stars.

Damien, damn him, stops right as I'm teetering on the cusp.

"Please," I beg, though I know it's futile.

He says nothing as he unstraps me, and though I don't stand—he hasn't told me I can—I stretch the kinks out of my muscles as he goes to the bar, then returns with a shot of bourbon on ice for me. I toss it back, enjoying the burn, then meet his eyes. "Are we almost there?"

"No." He takes the seat next to me, then starts to unzip his slacks. "Come here, baby. I want those lips on my cock."

I do as he says, relishing the feel of him, the taste of him. Enjoying the way his hand twines in my hair, guiding my motion. I'm deliciously wet, the insides of my thighs slick, and I press my legs together as my sex pulses, craving what my mouth has.

"And Masque?" Damien says, as if we were still on the same sex club conversation from earlier. "I know you remember that."

I don't answer—my mouth is otherwise occupied, and the pressure on my head makes it clear he doesn't need or want a reply. He knows well enough that I remember. The private Beverly Hills sex club is owned by a friend—Hollywood mogul and well-known bad boy Matthew Holt—and we went to his club not long before the horror with Anne began.

We went further there. Not entirely public sex, but Damien had led me to a second story alcove, from which we could look down and see the masked strangers engaged in every manner of intimate act below us. We'd been turned on, both by the surroundings and the knowledge that though many in the club switched partners, that was the one thing we would never do.

Before, in Paris, he'd said he would never let another man see me. But that was years ago, and Damien is a man who likes to show off what belongs to him. He'd released the tie at my neck, letting my halter-style top fall, baring my breasts to anyone who might look up. And though they couldn't see the rest of it, he bent me over, lifted the back of my skirt, and fucked me from behind.

It had been wild. Decadent. And one of the more erotic things we've ever done together. There's always a risk where Damien is concerned. Of being recognized. Of intimate pictures being released to the press. Both clubs have a strict privacy policy, and yet there is always that fear.

I'd conquered the fear those nights. Conquered, and embraced it. Even turned it around and let it fuel my desire, adding another layer of eroticism to my already intensely aroused state.

That's what he's doing now, I realize. That's why he's said we're going back there. This trip—this game—is all about facing my fears.

And since I'm looking forward to this second visit to the Paris club, I can't help but think that it's working.

"Do you remember how exposed we felt at both clubs? How much it excited you?" Again, he doesn't expect my response, but he's voicing the things I've been thinking. "I wonder what you would do if we took the hidden part out of the equation. If I pushed this button to unlock the door, switching the light to green. If I called Katie over the intercom and asked her to bring me a drink."

I've gone completely still. Surely he wouldn't really…

"I think I'd like to sip a bourbon while my beautiful wife sucks me off. What do you think?" he asks, releasing his grip on my hair. "Should I call her?"

I lift my head, trying to calm my pounding heart. "You're not making me afraid," I lie. "I know you won't let Katie in."

"Won't I? We've been pushing boundaries, sweetheart. And so far, we've both enjoyed every step forward we've taken."

I open my mouth, but can think of nothing to say. I'll admit there's something enticing about the fantasy of being watched. Of being secretly caught out doing something naughty. But I'm not about to admit that to Damien. And Katie is not on my imaginary audience list.

"Come here," he says as he urges me onto his lap. I rock my hips, enjoying the feel of his cock at my entrance, then cry out at the wonderful sensation of my husband filling me as he holds my hips and forces me down. I arch back, wanting even more of him. Wanting all of this man I adore. This man who pushes my limits even while holding me close.

I move against him, my own private lap dance, trying to take him even deeper. I'm watching his face, the way his eyes darken as passion overwhelms him. And I'm listening to his low, rasping groans as he grows even harder inside me, coming closer and closer to exploding.

His hand moves to the call button, his finger hovering just over it. He's bluffing. I'm certain.

My certainty dims as his finger starts to lower. I bite my lip, afraid I've misjudged him. And, dear God, I do not want Katie to find us like this, because how the hell would I be able to fly with her again?

"Damien..."

"I'm going to push the button, baby. I told you I was going to push you, didn't I?"

"I—I could say sunset." The words blurt out of me, and he freezes at the mention of our safeword.

"You could," he says. "Are you going to?"

"I—I—" I draw in a breath, then gather my courage. "No," I finally say, not because I want Katie to come in, but because I don't want Damien to know he's reached my limit. He wants me to face my fears? If that's what he thinks I need, then, goddammit, I'm going to trust my husband.

"No," I repeat more firmly, then hold my breath, waiting.

He doesn't push it. Instead, he pulls his hand away. "I'm not going to push it," he says, and I sag with relief. "You are."

"What?"

"You heard me. Are you afraid?"

"Yes. No. Embarrassed," I say, finally corralling my emotions.

"That's a type of fear. A fear that people will look at you a certain way. Think of you a certain way. A fear that you've acted outside the accepted parameters."

"Yeah, well, that applies to me," I say as he slips his hand between our joined bodies.

"Baby, you're so fucking wet. I think you like it."

"The fantasy," I admit. "Not reality."

He says nothing, but he slides his finger between us, making it slick. Then he reaches behind me, teasing my ass with his fingertip, making me suck in an excited breath as he enters me.

"You like this," he whispers and I whimper in acknowledgement. "Hold my shoulders," he demands. "Rock your hips. Ride me hard. Your ass, your cunt. I own every bit of you, Nikki. Tell me."

"You own me." I have to work to get out the words. He's deep inside me, hitting that magical spot with both his finger and his cock, and pushing me so close—so incredibly fucking close.

"Please, Damien. I need—"

"Do you want me to tease your clit? Push you that last little bit over?" With his free hand, he does just that. As light as the brush of a butterfly wing, but the effect on my body is astounding. It pushes me to the edge, but not quite over, and I'm so ready, so turned on that I don't know if I can even survive the next few minutes if he doesn't give me that release.

"Please," I beg.

"Push the button," he whispers, and I'm too far gone to even be shocked by his words. "Forget embarrassment, forget fear. Forget everything but the pleasure I can give you. Push the button if you want to come."

I'm beyond caring. Hell, I'm beyond thinking. I want release. I want to satisfy Damien.

I want to prove to him I can fight my fears.

Most of all, I want him to take me over.

I push the button. And the moment I do, he increases the pressure to my clit. I press my lips together, fighting a scream of deep pleasure as I shake with the force of the orgasm, my body clenching so tight around his finger and cock it's a wonder I don't cut off his blood flow.

I don't care about anything but riding this out, about absorbing the pleasure that he's giving me.

And then I hear the electronic ding that signals the opening of the door from the galley into the passenger side.

It's like a splash of cold water, and I grip his shoulders, trying to bring myself back down to earth. I *am* embarrassed, but that's okay. I can handle it. Damien's my husband after all, and the fact that we have a sex life is hardly breaking news.

I bite my lip as I glance at Damien's stoic expression. He's looking over my shoulder, and I twist at the waist to look behind me, expecting to see Katie shocked into stillness.

But there's no one.

For a second, I'm confused. "You rigged it. Katie never saw the call. And the door never unlocked."

He lifts a shoulder in silent confession, and I realize in that moment that some part of me knew it. Because I know Damien, and he knows my limits.

But maybe my limits are inching out. Slowly, I think. But maybe I'm getting bolder. More fearless.

The bottom line, of course, is that I pushed the button—and he made sure that if I did, absolutely nothing would happen. I flash a triumphant grin. "I guess that makes *you* the one who's afraid," I tease.

"Careful. We still have most of a transatlantic flight to go. Who knows what else I'll come up with?"

I ease off of him, my body tingling. "I think we should go to the state room and explore all the various possibilities." I let my gaze dip to his still-hard cock. "Sir," I add with a devious smile.

"And I think that's one of the best ideas I've heard in a very long time."

Chapter Seven

It's just past one in the afternoon when we land at an executive airport on the outskirts of Paris. It takes hardly any time to deal with all the administrative details surrounding international travel, and soon enough we're in one of the Stark International limos, and the driver is whisking us to our hotel.

I settle back beside Damien and watch the sights of Paris flash by. When we were here for our honeymoon, Damien booked us into a charming little hotel on the rue du Faubourg Saint-Honoré. He'd told me that he wanted us to disappear, and so he'd selected a small hotel that was absolutely stunning—and entirely unconnected to Stark International.

This trip, however, is all about work, and so the limo whisks us from the airport to the Stark Century Paris, located on the Place Vendôme, right across from the historic Ritz Paris hotel.

As far as I'm concerned, the travel details are the best part of being Mrs. Damien Stark. Everything from private planes to hotel limos to the ease of checking in. I've enjoyed those perks since my first days with Damien, but today they are lifesavers. I am, after all, still wearing nothing but a trench coat, and though I may have been self-conscious in the chopper and initially in the Bombardier, I've settled into what is starting to feel like a permanent state of naughty arousal. I wouldn't have wanted to tug my luggage off of a baggage claim carousel—not with the lingering possibility of the belt loosening and the coat falling open—but I'm not above opening it myself in the privacy of our limo.

Damien, however, doesn't take the bait.

On the contrary, when I sit across from him, part my legs, and start to unbutton the coat, all he does is lift a brow and say, "No."

"No?" I repeat.

He studies me. "Then again, you do look appetizing. Do you want me to order you to open the coat? To spread your legs the way you did in the plane? Do you want me to watch while you finger yourself, teasing your clit until you explode for me?"

I whimper. I honestly hadn't thought that far ahead, but what he is saying sounds pretty damn good to me. "Yes, Sir. Yes, please."

"That would be nice. I like seeing you hot. Aroused. Wanting me. I like the way your skin flushes before you come, the way your nipples tighten and your lips part. I like knowing how wet you get exposing yourself to me. And after you've gone over the edge, I love the way your cunt feels around my cock when I fuck you all the way to another, bigger orgasm."

He pauses, and I swallow, realizing my mouth is painfully dry.

"Do you like all that too, baby?"

"Yes," I whisper.

"Good. Now tighten the sash on your coat and remember that on this trip, I'm the one who decides when and where and how. Not you."

A flash of anger cuts through me, but it's underscored by an even deeper arousal. And though I won't admit it if he asks—not easily, anyway—I can't deny to myself how much I like this game he's playing.

I resign myself to watching the city go by, then draw in an

awestruck breath as we approach the Place Vendôme and I see the famous column originally erected by Napoleon.

The Stark Century and a few of the other buildings that line this historic square were created from several of the magnificent residences that once graced the area. The whole square is breathtaking, but the entrance to the hotel has such a regal quality to it that for a moment I have to stop and simply absorb the stunning façade that is part of the history and beauty of this lovely city.

We're escorted inside, bypassing the checkout process in the elegant lobby. Just as well, I think, as I notice a tall man with white-blond hair arguing about something with a calm-looking clerk, who obviously has more patience than I do. Really not the kind of vibe I want spoiling the mood of our afternoon. And whatever the guy's problem is, I'm sure Damien's staff will handle it brilliantly.

I force my attention away from the reception desk and return it to the interior of the lobby. The intricate woodwork. The stunning art. The glass cases showcasing the incredible jewelry on sale in the various mezzanine-level stores. I try not to gawk— after all, as Damien's wife, I should be used to this kind of luxury. And to an extent I am. But the history and beauty that now surrounds us takes my breath away.

We're led up two flights of stairs to a luxury suite with three bedrooms, four baths, a living room, a sitting room, a dining room, three bars, a library, and a gorgeous, huge balcony that looks out over an interior courtyard.

There is no kitchen, and I realize that's because the staff will jump to our every culinary whim. There's already a welcome plate with wine, cheese and chocolate on the coffee table in the sitting room.

The best part is the closets that, as the manager shows me, are already stocked with our clothes. Damien keeps a set of outfits stored in the hotel for his frequent trips, and the staff routinely brings his cases to the suite before his arrival and unpacks. I don't have a secondary wardrobe, but someone purchased a number of outfits for me, per Damien's instructions.

As soon as the manager leaves, I explore, absolutely delighted. "This place is amazing. I'm going to come with you on all your trips from now on."

"I don't usually stay in this suite," he tells me. "But you're welcome any time." He smiles indulgently as I peek into every nook and cranny, and he lets me enjoy the suite for a full ten minutes before calling me to him. I stand in front of him, grinning. "I'm enjoying our trip so far."

"Good," he says. "Take off the coat."

I comply quickly, anticipating his touch. I've been in an almost constant state of sexual excitement since we left the resort, and it's been even more intense since the jet. Honestly, I haven't been this aware of the heat between my legs since before I got pregnant with Ashley, the baby girl I miscarried before we adopted Lara.

Not that I've been unsatisfied with Damien recently—far, far from it. But this reminds me of our early months together, when my body seemed permanently, constantly aroused.

"You're smiling," he says. "Tell me what you're thinking."

"That I like the way you make me feel."

"How's that?"

I meet his eyes. "Like any minute you're going to fuck me."

He holds out his hand. "Come with me."

I take it eagerly, and he leads me to the bedroom. He nods to the bed, then tells me to get on. I do, then turn to look at him, only to find him pulling a tie from the bureau drawer.

For a moment, I expect that he intends to use it on me. Then he hangs it around his collar, studies himself in the dresser mirror, and begins to expertly knot it.

"What—"

"I have a meeting, remember?"

I pull my knees up, hugging them to my chest, my back to the headboard. "But I thought—"

"Thinking's my job this trip, Ms. Fairchild," he says, looking at me in the mirror's reflection. "Try to keep that in mind."

I begin to speak, then change my mind. He watches me, then continues to knot his tie. When he's finished, he turns. "You should get comfortable," he says, in a tone that makes clear that's an order and not a suggestion. "Take a nap. And stay in bed. I want you rested tonight."

I perk up a bit at that. My disappointment still lingers, but I do realize that this trip didn't originally include me. And I allow myself to cling to the anticipation of the night to come.

"Actually," he says, with a devious gleam in his eye, "let me help you get comfortable."

He crosses the room in two long strides, then positions me in the center of the bed, my legs spread wide.

I consider telling him that this isn't an ideal napping place, but at the same time I know that this situation is rife with erotic possibilities. I weigh speaking against eroticism, then stay silent. Proving once again that, push comes to shove, sex wins out over reason in almost all situations.

He binds my legs to the bedposts using two coils of rope that I'm pretty sure he brought from our bungalow at the resort. He chooses not to bind my arms, though, telling me that he's keeping my hands free in case I want to adjust the blanket he also left for me.

I consider pointing out that I can simply sit up and bend over to untie the leg restraints, but I say nothing. I'm sure he already knows that. And if he doesn't … well, it's not really my job to tell him, is it?

* * * *

"Did you get out of bed?"

Damien's voice startles me, and I struggle up onto my elbows, blinking into the dark hotel room. "I—What?"

"I asked if you got out of bed."

"No, sir," I say.

"No?" His brows rise, and I silently curse. He's caught me out. Of course he's caught me out. "Care to try again?"

I lick my lips. "I had to pee."

"Did I tell you to stay in the bed?"

"Yes, sir."

"And did you leave the bed?"

I sigh. "Yes, sir."

He sits on the edge of the mattress. "Then you can obviously unstrap yourself. Do that, and then I want you over my knee."

"You're going to spank me?" Already, my body is reacting. My sex aching from the mere thought of his hand smacking hard against my ass before his palm gently soothes the sting. Even the thought makes me wet, but that's nothing compared to how aroused I know I'll be when my ass is red and stinging. That's when he'll finger fuck me, thrusting deep and hard while ordering me to come for him, to explode for him. And after I do, he'll lay me gently on the bed and take me all over again.

So, yeah, I don't really hesitate.

"Five," he says. And true to his word, he lands five solid smacks to my rear, each one followed by his palm on my reddening ass, the gentle rubbing motions meant to soothe.

With each spank, I get wetter and wetter, until he finally stops. I hold my breath, expecting the exquisite sensation of his fingers deep inside me.

Except there is no touch. No tease. No anything.

All he does is tell me to get dressed.

For a moment, I consider arguing. Even begging. Because it's almost embarrassing how profound my disappointment is.

Then I remember what he told me on the plane—that after his meeting he was taking me to À la Lune. And that, I think, will definitely take the edge off.

Chapter Eight

"Wear this," Damien says, handing me a pale pink shift that I have to pull on over my head.

Although my thighs are still slick with my arousal, he's refused to let me wash up, and underwear is out of the question as well.

Even so, the dress is modest enough, though my rock-hard nipples are obvious through the thin silk, and the cut is such that it hugs my body a little too closely, outlining the curve of my ass and revealing the V of my sex when I walk. I know, because I made a point of walking in front of the mirror, and this dress definitely wouldn't be in my wardrobe back home in LA.

Still, considering where we're heading, I think it's more than appropriate. But, of course, it turns out that isn't where we're going at all. At least, not right away.

Instead, we walk the short distance down the Rue du Castiglione toward the Jardin des Tuileries. We cross the Rue de Rivoli and enter the park. I hadn't bothered to check the time, but the park is thinning out. It closes at nine, and I assume we're getting close to that time. For the first time, I wonder how long Damien had been back in the hotel before he woke me.

When we reach the park's center promenade, we turn left. In the distance, the Louvre museum stands majestically in front of us, and we continue toward it, the glass pyramid that marks its entrance glowing in the dimming light. "Where are we going?" I ask, and when he tells me that we're going to dinner at the Louvre, I almost beg him to let me go back to the hotel and change.

I don't, though. For one, I know he'd say no. For another, the dress is fine—it's just not entirely appropriate. And whatever else I might be afraid of, having people stare at me because of my attire is low on the list.

It turns out we don't dine inside the museum itself, but in Café Marly, located beneath the arcade of the Louvre's Richelieu wing. We sit on the outdoor terrace, which provides a stunning view of the pyramid, brilliantly illuminated in the deepening night.

I expect him to tease me sexually. To insist that I pull the dress up and sit with my bare ass on the seat despite the fact that our table has no cloth. Or that he'll slide his arm around my shoulders and stroke his thumb casually over my nipple for anyone who is dining to see.

But he does none of that. Instead, he orders for us, and we spend a lovely two hours finishing off an incredible bottle of wine and indulging in duck foie gras, rack of lamb, and an absolutely marvelous *mille-feuille*. The latter, which we call a Napoleon back in the States, is one of my favorite pastries, and this one is about the best I've ever put in my mouth.

All in all, it's a wonderful dinner date with my husband, and my only disappointment is that Damien seems to have entirely forgotten tonight's original plan. Even when the plates are cleared and we're finishing the last of our coffee and brandy, he doesn't mention the club at all.

Instead, he pays the bill, extends his hand to help me up, and guides me out of the restaurant.

I consider saying something, but this entire trip is Damien's show, and we talk quietly about Paris, sights he wants to show me while we're in town, and similar travel-related conversation. On any other trip, I'd be fully engaged. Now, I'm wondering what game he's playing.

It's not until we've actually stepped inside the hotel that he pauses, then turns to look at me directly, his head cocked. "You haven't said a word. Should I assume you're relieved that we're not going to the club?"

"We're not?" I hear the disappointment in my voice, and Damien must as well, considering the way he's smiling.

"That depends. It won't be like last time," he says. "Are you prepared?"

I raise a brow. "You're asking me? I thought this whole exercise was about pushing my limits. Facing my fears."

He doesn't answer. His small smile is enough, because it tells me that he has something intense planned. And he's giving my imagination the full length of the ride to the club to imagine every decadent possibility.

"With me," he says, then leads me back through the doors where a limo is now waiting for us. We get in, and I notice my trench coat is laying across one of the seats. I swallow, wondering...

As soon as we are underway, he orders me to strip.

"I—"

I don't finish the sentence. Damien's look of approbation cuts me off too quickly. Instead, I pull the shift up over my head, then sit back as Damien looks me up and down, my skin tingling from the intensity of his gaze. "You are so damn beautiful," he says. "How can I not show you off?"

My heart lurches in my chest. The first time we came to À la Lune, he'd specifically told me that he didn't want me naked, though many of the other guests—men and women—were. He said he didn't intend to share even the sight of me.

But a lot has changed since our honeymoon, and I wonder what additional boundaries he wants to push tonight. The possibility that he wants me bare in the club scares me, and I consider what I'll do. I can call sunset—he will never push me past my safeword. Or I can trust that he is right. That I'll survive the embarrassment and the fear that—despite the club's strict vetting of its members and even stricter rules about privacy and no photography—some image of me will make it into the tabloids.

What if it did?

That would be hell, no doubt about that. But would it ruin my marriage? My friendships?

I know that it wouldn't.

What about my kids? It wouldn't be easy, but they're young enough now to not even notice, and by the time they are old enough to care, the tabloids would have moved on. If they dig it out at some point, though…well, it wouldn't be my first choice of a conversation to have with my kids, but I would survive.

So would my business, if any of my clients get wind of the photos. It would be awkward and strange, but the bottom line is that this trip is about trust and fear. And if Damien wants to push me that way, I trust him…and I can overcome my fear.

He is still watching me, and I draw a breath. "Is this how you want me in the club? Should I wear the trench coat for the walk from the limo to the door?"

"Is that what you want?"

I meet his eyes straight on. "I want what you want."

"Not afraid?"

"I'm afraid," I admit, then lift my chin. "But I'm yours. I won't argue."

He cups my cheek, then kisses me gently. "You're amazing, Mrs. Stark."

I smile up at him, knowing that the title is one more way of claiming me.

He opens a compartment behind the bench on which we're sitting, and pulls out a white box, like the kind his shirts come in. He hands it to me, and when I open it, I find a blue strapless dress made of the thinnest of material. It has a slit up one thigh, and nothing but an elastic band to keep it in place above my breasts.

"Put it on," he orders, and when I do I realize that although it is sheer, the swirls of blue are placed strategically, so that the darker areas cover my breasts and sex. I wouldn't wear it to the grocery store, but for this club, I will be more covered than most.

"Can I wear this in there? I thought they provided sarongs."

"For those who want them." He lifts the last bit of tissue out of the box. "You'll wear this, too," he says revealing two black masks. Enough to keep our identity hidden from anyone who doesn't already know us—which, presumably, includes these French guests.

"We didn't wear masks last time," I point out. In fact, the only time we have was at Masque, when he took me on the balcony, where anyone who cared to look up could see.

"Last time, we watched from an alcove. This time, the only one I intend to watch is you."

My mouth goes dry, as his words have confirmed my suspicions, but I nod, take a deep breath, and try to calm the butterflies in my stomach. Butterflies that are borne of both nerves and a building sense of desire.

It's easy enough to enter the club. Damien is a member, having renewed that privilege before our honeymoon. He accepts a robe, then goes to change in the dressing room before leading me into the heart of the club. Unlike Masque, which has an elegant, cocktail party feel to it, this club makes me think of Roman orgies.

There are several rooms, many with hot tubs filled with naked men and women, some lost in their own passion, others who watch as Damien and I walk by. Most days, I would assume that it's Damien they're watching. That confident walk, that godlike body. But tonight, I know that it is me. Several of the walls are mirrored, and I've seen my reflection. The gown allows for modesty, but not consistently. When the light hits it, even the dark blue areas turn transparent, giving anyone who's looking a glimpse of my body underneath. But, thank goodness, only a glimpse.

After doing the pageant circuit for so many years, I'm used to being on display. But this is different. And, strangely, not unpleasant.

"You like this," Damien says, his low voice rumbling through me. "The way they look at you. The hint of your body they see when the light is just right."

"I do," I admit, holding my head high.

"Why? Tell me what it is that excites you."

I glance down, my gaze directed to my arm, and his light grip on my bare flesh. "I like that they know I belong to you. I like that it makes me proud."

"Baby," he says, his voice low and full of heat and promise. He tugs me into a curtained alcove, across from which a woman is laid out naked on a bench, a man's face buried between her thighs.

I tremble, watching the two of them from this secluded place, through filmy curtains that hide less than my dress. Damien moves behind me, then tugs down the top of my dress so that he can cup my bare breasts. I breathe in sharply, then sharper still when he moves even closer and I feel the press of his erection against my lower back.

"Tell me what you see," he demands, as the fingers of one hand tighten on my nipple and the other snakes down to slip inside the slit of this barely-there dress. His fingers dance lightly over my clit, and I gasp as heat sizzles between my sex and my nipple, a wild passion rising. A wanton need. "Nikki," he urges. "Tell me."

"She's close." I'm watching the way the woman arches up. The curve of her neck, the shape of her back. She's shifting her hips, as if that will guide him to that sweet, sweet spot. I imagine it's me on that bench, Damien's tongue on me, so intimate and yet so open, my pleasure there for anyone to see.

"What else?"

"She's close, but he's teasing her." I can feel her desire, and I hear it reflected in my voice. "She wants it to last as much as she wants to go over."

The woman's eyes are open, and for a moment they land on me. I see a hint of a smile before a fresh wave of fire crashes through her and she arches up, her moans echoing in the small room.

"She knows we're watching," I tell Damien, then turn in his arms so that my breasts are pressed against his still cinched robe. "She likes it."

His lips brush over mine as he shifts his hands, easing my skirt up. He cups my ass, then slides one hand lower, easing between my legs to find my core. Slowly—so deliciously slowly—he eases to fingers inside me. I draw in a breath, then move my hips, slowly riding his fingers. "You like it, too," he murmurs, his lips brushing the side of my neck, causing a zillion sparks to crackle through me.

"Do you remember what I told you last time? When you asked why it turned you on so much?"

"Because they're a mirror," I say. "They reflect back my own desires."

His fingers slip out of me, and I moan in protest, only to be silenced when he spins me around and kisses me gently before stepping back and taking my hands. "Come with me," he says, and before I can protest that the top of my dress is still gathered around my waist, he leads us past the curtains.

"Damien!" I cry, tugging him to a stop.

His eyes meet mine, his brows rising in question.

"What are you doing?"

A hint of a smile touches his mouth as he says, "Let's find out what it's like to be the mirror."

* * * *

He leads me through the dim lights, past other couples, threesomes, and more. Some corners filled with passion. Some with punishment. And with each person, I wonder how it would feel if Damien was touching me that way, or that, or even like *that*.

He leads me into a room illuminated with dim red bulbs. Appropriate, I think. We pass several other couples as he takes me to a wooden bench. It's sitting a few feet from a wall, facing it, so that anyone on the bench has their back to the room.

"Shall I bend you over the back of that bench?" he asks. "Tie your arms to the slats. Stroke my hand between your thighs and tease your ass until you beg me to take you like that with the whole room watching?"

I open my mouth, then close it again when I realize my automatic reply was, "Yes."

He's watching my face, and I'm certain that he sees the truth in my eyes. But he doesn't call me on it. Instead, he takes my hand, circles the bench, and sits. He opens his robe, revealing his incredible body and fully erect cock. I know that I'm the only one who can see him. The bench is on one side of the wall, and all the other people are behind him. If they see anything, it's his still-robed shoulders and back.

But they can see me. I'm standing topless in front of him, the rest of my dress mostly sheer in the strange lighting.

I taste blood and realize I'm biting my lower lip.

"Nikki," Damien says softly, his hand extended. "Come here."

I do, and his touch gives me courage. "Why are we out here?" I ask.

"So you can watch them over my shoulder," he says, tugging me onto his lap, then he lifts my skirt so that he can hold my hips and guide me onto his rock-hard cock. "And so they can watch us, too."

I bite my lip hard, astounded that we're doing this. "Hold my shoulders, baby," he demands, and I comply, reminding myself that I'm masked as I look at the others in the room. Some uninterested, some watching. And in the eyes of everyone watching us, I see a heat at least equal to our own.

"Damien," I murmur, not sure what I'm feeling. Excitement or embarrassment. Fear or euphoria. All I know is that my body is on fire and my husband is so hard and filling me so deliciously.

His hands cup my ass, helping to thrust harder, deeper, and damned if I'm not wonderfully close, the edge of the universe rising up to greet me.

"Take off your mask."

His whispered words shock me even as an unexpected trill of excitement runs up my spine, making my core clench tight around his erection. "Damien, no. Someone will recognize me." I'm looking over his shoulder at the other couples and threesomes in this room. Couples in more compromising positions than we are. Some glance our way, but it's obvious they are lost in their own pleasure. Most don't even know we exist, too lost in a sexual haze.

Maybe it would be safe. But even so...

I moan as his hands on my hips push me, driving his cock deeper inside me. His dark eyes look into mine, full of heat and temptation and promise. And love. "Are you calling sunset?" I hear the effort it takes him to get out the words and I know he's close to exploding.

"I—" My mouth is so dry I can't get the words out. I want— God, I want—and yet...

"Think about the worst thing that could happen." His hand slips from my hips to my ass, his finger moving to trace intimately between my ass cheeks, making me rock and moan, wanting him deeper. Wanting him every way possible. Just *wanting* him.

His voice is low. Intimate. This conversation is meant for no one other than us. "Then ask yourself if you could survive that. You're afraid, Nikki. Conquer the fear."

He's right. It would be hell if I was recognized. I've had the tabloids after me, and it's horrible. But I've always survived. Always, because Damien was at my side.

I can get past my fear. I can own it. Use it. Turn it around and take power from it.

I think of those damn boys in the car. Of the way I took a blade to my skin during the worst of Anne's kidnapping. Of every time I let fear slide in and grab me by the throat.

No more.

I reach for the strap of my mask, but before I can take it off, Damien stills my hand.

"What are you—"

His grin has a hint of irony. "All I wanted was for you to learn to conquer your fear. That's far enough to see that you can. It's one thing to give in to fear. It's another to be reckless."

I nod, relieved. But at the same time, I raise a brow. "In other words, Mr. Stark, I'm braver than you."

"I suppose you are. What do you intend to do about that?"

I draw in a breath, then glance around the room. Anonymous bodies still move in the dark. I can smell the lust, the passion. And damned if I don't want to be part of it. "I'm going to fuck my husband," I say, moving my hips in time with my words, holding his gaze as I bring him back to full arousal.

"Oh, baby," he says, his hands on my hips as he guides me harder and deeper. "I love the way you surprise me."

I hook my hand around the back of his neck and rock my hips as my mouth meets his, my tongue going as deep as his cock. My other hand is on his bare chest for balance, and I can feel the tempo of his heart, the quickening as he comes closer, and the knowledge that he's as excited as I am makes me even wilder. "Please," I whisper. "Damien, please make me come."

He groans, sliding one hand between our bodies to find my clit. He teases me, his fingers working magic as I arch back, overwhelmed at the storm spinning out of control inside me. At the power of owning this moment and the knowledge that Damien is right there with me, holding fast to me as we inch beyond anywhere we've gone before. And God knows we've come far.

He breathes my name, then bends forward, his mouth closing over my breast, his teeth grazing my nipple as his free hand cups the back of my head, making it impossible for me to arch back too far, so that I have no choice but to look at the other lovers in this room if I open my eyes.

The room smells of sex, and the red tint that illuminates our bodies is like the reflection of our passion. His hands upon me act like a closed circuit, and my body explodes around his. My sex tightens, clenching his cock, claiming him as he readjusts his hands, once again taking my hips and slamming me down on to him, harder and harder until finally, sweetly, he explodes inside me and our joint exalted cries echo over the other bodies writhing in this small, dim room.

I cling to him, breathing hard, both our bodies relaxing together. Finally, he picks me up and carries me to a private chamber with nothing in it but the freshly-made bed where he gently deposits me, then tugs my dress the rest of the way off.

"I love you," he says simply, as he removes the robe and slides onto the duvet beside me.

"I know," I say. "That love is my strength." With a sigh, I curl up next to him, relishing the feel of his skin against mine. "I feel like we went to hell together and came out again through the fire. I feel raw. New." I smile at him. "I feel wonderful."

"Then my plan worked."

I laugh. "When don't your plans work?" I shift on the bed and sit up, facing him. "Do you remember when I told you that you couldn't control the world?"

"I believe you've mentioned it once or twice. You've said that I can't control the world, but I can control you."

I meet his eyes. "I was right. You *can* control me."

I see a flicker of confusion, and then he says, "You're saying it worked, bringing you here. Our game."

I nod. "I believed you before—when you said I was strong.

But then I cut again, and ... and I guess it felt as if everything that came before was erased. That I was weak after all."

"You know better. Everybody breaks a little sometime."

"And that doesn't make you weak. It makes you wounded." I squeeze his hand. "You told me that. You were right."

"I do love hearing that," he says, then kisses my fingertips. "I'll give you a choice. I can release you from our arrangement. We can go back to the hotel, get in bed, drink wine, watch a movie, and make love."

"Or?"

"Or we can stay here a few more hours. After that, we can continue as we've been during the rest of the trip. Maybe longer. I'll explore your fears. I'll push your boundaries."

"More than you already have?"

He only smiles.

"That," I say, an exultant anticipation already rising inside me. "Door Number Two."

He studies me. "Why?"

"Because I love you. Because I trust you. Because we haven't reached our limit yet."

"Limit?"

"Of what's enticing, exciting. Of what turns us on. We're still climbing the mountain, Damien. I want to know what it feels like when we reach the top."

"I'd say the view's pretty good from where we are," he says, his eyes skimming over every inch of me.

I move over, then straddle his waist. "The view's amazing."

"But you want more."

"No, I don't want more. I want all. All of you."

"You already have me."

"I know," I say happily. "And that's why I'm not afraid."

Chapter Nine

"Are you sure you don't want to join us, Tony?" I ask, using the nickname that Antonio Santos requested when we were introduced. I, of course, invited him to call me Nikki.

He smiles at me, but shakes his head. About thirty-five, he has the dark hair and warm brown skin that reflects his Mexican heritage. He also has the fresh, clean-cut appearance of a young businessman, a façade that camouflages all the rough edges that Damien swears make him such a viable candidate for Stark Security.

"I appreciate the offer, but I believe I'm otherwise engaged."

I turn, following the direction of his gaze, and note the leggy redhead who's been eyeing him throughout the entire meal. Damien and I share an amused glance before I turn back to Tony. "Looks like it," I say, and his eyes dance with amusement.

"I'm very happy we had the chance to meet. Your husband is excellent company, but you definitely brightened up the afternoon."

"Flirting?" Damien says, his voice laced with humor.

"With Damien Stark's wife? Would you be trying to hire me if I was that stupid?"

Damien chuckles. "Good point."

Damien and I met Tony for lunch at the hotel's restaurant as part of Damien's continuing effort to get the former Deliverance member to join the Stark Security team. Now, lunch is over, and Damien and I head through the lobby to our waiting car so that we can squeeze in a quick visit to the Rodin Museum before his final meeting of the day.

As we climb in, I see a tall man with a familiar shock of white-blond hair. I can't place him, but he snarls something at the doorman who's speaking to him, shoots a harsh glance toward our car, and then stalks off down the sidewalk.

"What?" I ask, realizing Damien has said something.

"I asked what you thought of Tony."

"I like him. And he seems to like you. Why is he hesitating?" The lunch was casual, a chance to interact informally, and we barely discussed business at all.

"Let's just say he's on a personal mission."

"But he worked with Deliverance," I point out.

"He did. His mission lined up well with Dallas's." Dallas Sykes started Deliverance to find the men who had kidnapped him and his sister as teenagers.

"Tony was kidnapped," I guess. "And he wanted to find his kidnapper."

"Not exactly. He was kidnapped, but he knew by whom. His father kidnapped him when he was seven and took him to Mexico City."

"His poor mother. Did she get him back?"

"She killed herself," Damien says and I shiver. "At least, that's what Tony's father told him."

"He doesn't believe that?"

Damien shrugs. "I don't think he wants to."

I take Damien's hand and squeeze, thinking of Anne, and how I might have lost her forever. "So he grew up with a father who kidnapped him. When did he learn the truth?"

"Actually, he was rescued and adopted by his uncle when he

was ten. And apparently, *rescued* is accurate. His father sounds worse than mine."

"I'm glad he got away."

"As am I. He hasn't specifically told me as much, but I think he's investigating his mother's death. And I know he's trying to find the man who gunned down his uncle."

My hand goes to my mouth, and I think of how much Antonio Santos has endured. And how focused he is now. How ready and able to face the world despite seeing so much horror in the world. "I hope he finds answers," I say. "But more, I hope he's able to move on."

"My thoughts exactly," Damien agrees.

It's not a long ride to the museum, and I think that I might come back later with my camera. The building itself is gorgeous, a former mansion where Rodin worked when he was in the city. Apparently, he donated much of his work and the artwork he collected, and now it fills the gardens and the interior of the rococo mansion.

We go inside first and wander leisurely. I love seeing the various pieces, including the famous The Kiss. But it's the art students that litter the floor that draw my attention. They seem to come in two varieties —lone wolves or those that travel in packs with their teacher as the leader. Armed with sketchpads, they are everywhere, leaning against walls, seated on the floor around statues. Their pencils move over pads as their eyes move back and forth between their own work and the genius that is Rodin. They've come here to be close to talent. To genius. To soak it in, to study, to analyze. And, yes, to envy.

There's a look in their eyes I recognize, because I've seen it in the eyes of the young men and women who work with Damien. With Jackson, too. The passion and talent of those two men is electrifying, and people are drawn to them like moths to a burning flame.

I glance sideways at my husband, seeing him instead of the art. And in that moment, I know that I am the luckiest woman on earth.

"Nikki?" The teasing tone draws me from my thoughts, and I look up to find Damien smiling at me. "You look mesmerized."

I study his face and nod. "Yeah," I say. "I am."

He takes my arm, oblivious to the full meaning of my words, and leads me outside. It's as if we've stepped into a magical world, with the stunning landscaping beneath the blue Parisian sky.

The Thinker sits in the garden to the right of the building, the massive Gates of Hell to the left, beautiful and fascinating despite the dark subject. Damien and I spend some time getting close to those famous doors, looking at the intricate detail of this intricate and disturbing piece.

But it's when we move behind the mansion that I really fall in love. There's sculpture in the garden, of course, but it is the simplicity of the manicured lawn that sings to my soul. A stunning grassy rectangle leading from the back stone patio all the way down to a small pond.

"Can you imagine the lawn parties this house must have seen?" I ask Damien. "Or the weddings." I imagine the bride coming down the stairs, then walking a rolled-out carpeted path to her groom at the pond. "Wouldn't that be magnificent?"

He says nothing, but an odd expression colors his face. "Damien?"

"You're right," he says. "It's an incredible venue."

"I wish we had longer."

"I can send the car back for you," he tells me, but I decline. Instead, I join him as the car takes us on to the office building where Damien has his meeting, then returns me to the hotel.

Since I'm now in the mood to take pictures, I hurry inside. I grab my camera and return to the sidewalk, intending to walk the short distance to the Tuileries.

I don't get that far. As soon as I've rounded the corner, I'm slammed from behind. Fear and confusion crash through me, but I don't even have time to react before my attacker spins me around and slams my back against a wall. It's broad daylight, but no one stops, and I think it's because my attacker is right in my face, so close we could be lovers.

It's the white-blond man, and his face is full of hate. "Your husband thinks he is better than everyone," he says in heavily accented English. "He thinks I am not good enough to work at his fucking hotel. Damien Stark with all his pretty things. Maybe I should make his wife a little bit less pretty. Do you think?"

My heard is pounding, but despite all my adrenaline, I can't struggle out of his grasp. I can think, though, and it's Damien who fills my mind as I jerk a knee up, aiming for his crotch.

He dodges, a deadly fury building in his eyes, and I fear that I just made a deadly mistake.

He snarls, and as he lunges forward, cold terror courses through me.

I have only a split second, and I force my panic down. I don't have time for fear; I only have time to fight. I clench my fist, then lash out, gaining momentum as I thrust up the way Damien does in our gym. My hand explodes with pain as I make contact with the underside of his chin, knocking his head back as he stumbles away from me.

I don't hesitate, just take off running, expecting to hear his footsteps behind me. Anticipating the sudden stop when he grabs the back of my shirt just inches before I reach the corner.

But there is no tug. And as I careen around the corner, I realize I'm free. I did it. I got away.

"Mrs. Stark!"

I barely register the distant words and keep on running.

"Nikki!" The voice is closer. "Wait!"

Tony.

Confused, I stop and turn, only to see him rounding the corner, too, my attacker held in a head lock.

"I wish I'd passed by sooner," he says calmly. "But from what I saw, you did just fine." He glances down at the guy with distaste. "Want me to take care of this garbage for you?"

Tony looks ready to pound the guy into mincemeat right there on the street, and I'm tempted to let him do it. I, however, have a better idea. "He's been loitering around the Stark Century. I say we let Damien handle it."

Tony laughs. "Nikki," he says with a grin. "I like the way you think."

* * * *

I bend forward, my eyes locked with Damien's as he moves inside me. I'm straddling him, watching the fear and fury slowly ease from his face.

He came the moment the hotel called, and once the attacker was off the premises and with the police, he aimed me upstairs.

"Nikki." The word seemed ripped from him as we entered our suite, and it still hung in the air when he pushed me back against the wall and claimed my mouth with his.

He's said nothing else since, but I know what he's thinking. What he's doing. He's thinking he could have lost me. And he's facing his fear the way that Damien does. By grabbing tight. In this case, to me.

I rock my hips as I feel the tension build inside both of us, recalling his anger when he learned that my attacker had been turned down for a job as a front desk clerk. He'd seen me with Damien, realized who I was, and decided to work out his frustrations.

Tony, thankfully, had just left the redhead. He'd been walking to his own hotel when he saw me break away and start running.

"If anything had happened to you—" Damien says now, flipping us over so that my back is to the mattress and my knees are bent. He's deep inside me. Claiming me. Facing the core of his biggest fear—losing me.

The thought both humbles and excites me, and I cling to Damien, urging him deeper, harder, until we are both lost in the motions of making love. Of claiming each other and burying our shared fears in passion.

Our orgasms come fast and hard, and afterwards, we lay twined together. "I'm so sorry, baby. I should have been there."

"I'm fine. I was scared, but I'm okay. And luckily Tony was around to catch him. Not a guy I'd like to know was running loose in Paris."

"Agree. I'd give him a raise if he worked for me."

I laugh and snuggle closer.

"I'm so proud of you," he whispers, brushing my temple with a kiss. "You were amazing."

"Thanks. And thanks for this trip. I'll never lose myself in that bubble again, and that's okay. I want to live in the real world, and not worry about all the dark clouds."

"You're not afraid anymore?"

"I'm not saying I'm one hundred percent, and I'll still go to counseling because it helps. But fear isn't going to get the better of me anymore. I'm stronger than I think I am, and a lot of that is because you're always with me, even when you're not."

"I am," he says. "Don't ever forget it."

"I won't. The truth is, I've always known it." I meet his eyes. "Thank you for bringing me here and reminding me."

* * * *

I have no idea how long I sleep, but I'm dreaming of the kids and breakfast when I wake, so disoriented I can smell bacon and hear the laughter of my girls.

Except...

I roll out of bed, tugging on the hotel robe that I'd thrown across a chair. I hurry down the long hallway and find my girls and Damien seated at the table by the window in the sitting room, a room-service catered buffet lining the opposite wall.

"Mommy!" Both girls cry out in unison, and Lara jumps off her chair and races toward me. Anne follows on her much shorter legs.

I bend to them and swoop them into my arms, kiss them fiercely, then raise my face to Damien, who looks ridiculously proud of himself. "Thank you," I say. "But how?"

He just grins as footsteps approach from behind us.

I turn to see Jamie and Ryan enter the room. "Best babysitting job ever," Jamie says. "Definitely count us in for schlepping your kids anywhere on the globe. So long as Damien provides the transportation."

"We flew on the jet, Mommy," Lara tells me. "Anne slept mostly, but I got to sit in the cockpit."

"You did. With Grayson?"

"No time to get Grayson there and back again," Damien tells me. "But we'll all go home with him together."

I grin, loving the sound of that.

"Can we 'splore, Daddy?" Lara asks, taking Anne's hand. She means explore, and it's her favorite thing to do in new places. I think she believes she'll find a secret passage to Narnia. And in one of Damien's properties, that kind of magic might be possible.

"I haven't been to Paris in ages," Jamie says, snagging a piece of bacon as the girls scamper. She uses it to indicate Ryan. "And even though he says we only did it as a favor to Damien, I saw him researching sex clubs on his phone during the flight."

"I think you're confusing my browser history with yours. Shall we compare?"

Jamie crosses her arms and stares him down. "Are you trying to tell me that *you* aren't interested in a sex club?"

I meet Damien's eyes; he looks as amused as I am.

Ryan's lips curve in the hint of a smile. "Kitten," he says, "I don't need to research."

She smacks him lightly on the shoulder. "All I can say is your knowledge better have been obtained before you married me."

He laughs, holding his hands up in surrender.

I raise a brow. "You guys are like an X-rated Ricky and Lucy."

Jamie cocks her head. "Funny. What about you two? Got any recommendations?"

I allow myself a small grin and a sideways glance at my husband. "We'll talk."

Chapter Ten

Damien leaned back on his elbows, his face to the sky. The sun was shining, flowers were blooming, his wife's head was resting on his stomach as she napped in the sun, and his two little girls were chasing each other around the picnic blanket and giggling like fiends.

He was soaking up the sun in Paris surrounded by his family, all happy and safe.

On the whole, life was pretty damn good.

He intended it to stay that way.

They'd come to the Tuileries after he and Ryan had squeezed in one more meeting with Antonio. "Your wife's an incredible woman," he'd said. "She didn't deserve that."

"No," Damien had agreed. "She didn't."

"But from what I saw, she was amazing. How's she doing now?"

"Good," Damien assured him. "Shaken, but fine." He'd smiled to himself when he'd added, "She's stronger than she seems. And stronger than she thinks."

"Most people are," Antonio had said. He'd paused, looking like he wanted to say something, but didn't know where to start. Damien gave him time, waiting until Antonio finally looked between him and Ryan and said, "Listen, Stark. Hunter. I like what you're doing, and you both seem like good guys. Dallas and Quincy vouch for you both, and that says a lot to me. But I can't sign on. Not now. I've got—well, I think you both know I've got things to do. But don't write me off, okay?"

"I wouldn't dream of it," Damien had said, glancing at Ryan with a subtle nod, at which point Ryan took the ball.

"Any time you change your mind, you say the word and you're in," Ryan told him. "And if you need help, Stark Security is there for you. Anytime. Anything."

Antonio leaned back with a chuckle. "Nice offer, but I won't hold you to it. You two might not have been listening to me when we met the other day. Let's just say that I want answers, and I don't mind cutting corners to get them."

"Do you think we don't understand that sometimes you have to push the envelope?" Damien asked. "Anytime. Anything. That's a promise."

"Okay." Antonio had said the word slowly, then extended his hand to both of them. "I'll be in touch."

Damien hoped he would. Stark Security needed people who weren't afraid to break the rules. Who knew how to get answers and how to help.

Ryan had left him after the meeting to pick up Jamie. They were off to explore the city before heading out for a tour of Versailles in the morning. Damien didn't envy them two days of walking. At the moment, he was more than content to relax on a blanket under the Parisian sky with his wife while his children ran and laughed and sang silly songs.

Today, the Stark family was hanging out, being lazy in the shadow of the Louvre. They deserved it.

He reached down, running his fingers through Nikki's golden hair, listening to her soft sighs.

"This day," he said. "If I could package this day, I'd make a fortune. But I wouldn't sell it."

Nikki turned her head, lifting a hand to shade her eyes.

"Because you already have a fortune?"

"I do," he said. "But I still want more."

"More money?"

"More of this. I'd keep it bottled up so that I always had this day. With you. With the girls."

Her smile lit her face. "Will you share the bottle with me?"

"Always."

"Good." She stretched, then sat up as Lara called from near the duck pond, "Mommy! Mommy, we want apple slices!"

"Duty calls," she said, then kissed him lightly before standing and rummaging in the wicker picnic basket that the hotel kitchen had packed for them.

He watched as she headed toward the pond, then sat with the girls. As Anne pointed at the ducks and Lara kept up a constant chatter, Nikki distributed apple slices, hugs, and kisses.

As for Damien, he simply watched, mesmerized by his family. By the swell of his heart when he looked at them, the pride he felt that Nikki was his—that this family was theirs—outweighing everything else he'd accomplished in this world.

He wondered if she fully understood what she was to him. If she realized that she was the core of his strength, even as she was his greatest weakness.

She came over to him, a teasing smile dancing on her lips as she offered him an apple slice. "You look like you're thinking deep thoughts. Everything okay?"

He took the fruit, then tugged on her wrist until she gave in and collapsed, laughing, into his arms.

He quieted her with a kiss, long and deep and deliciously sweet. "I'm great," he whispered when they broke the kiss. "How could I be anything else with you by my side?"

"Sweet talker."

"Truth teller." He studied her face, then took her hands in his. "Let's renew our vows."

She leaned back, clearly surprised. "Mr. Stark. Are you proposing?"

"I suppose I am. I thought about what you said. About how the yard at the Rodin Museum would be perfect for a wedding. I'm not saying we should do it there, but somewhere, and this time not just us."

"Regrets, Mr. Stark?"

He could tell from the curve of her mouth and the tease in her voice that she knew damn well he had no regrets around their elopement. But he didn't tease her back. He just said simply, "None."

She studied him, her eyes moving slightly as if she was reading the truth on his face. "What brought this on? Just the museum?"

"I think that planted a seed. Remembering the night at the club helped it bloom."

"À la Lune?" She sounded understandably confused.

"Don't worry. I want our renewal to be clothed. And G-rated," he added with a nod to the girls, who were twirling with their arms out, making themselves dizzy, then falling to the ground. "But I liked what you said."

"That we're still climbing the mountain."

He nodded. "We've reached a checkpoint, and now we're moving forward. Growing our family. Pushing our boundaries," he added with a devious grin. "The truth is, I renew all my promises to you with every kiss. Nikki, my love, I want to make it formal again. In front of our friends and our children."

He stood, then got down on one knee. "Nikki Fairchild Stark, will you do me the honor of marrying me again?"

Her bright smile filled his soul. "Mr. Stark," she said as she took his hands and pulled him up and into her arms, "it would be my absolute pleasure."

* * * *

Also from 1001 Dark Nights and J. Kenner, discover Damien, Hold Me, Tame Me, Tempt Me, Justify Me, Caress of Darkness, Caress of Pleasure, and Rising Storm.

* * * *

Charismatic. Dangerous. Sexy as hell.
Meet the elite team at Stark Security.

Shattered With You
Broken With You
Ruined With You
And more to come...

Sign up for the 1001 Dark Nights Newsletter
and be entered to win a Tiffany Key necklace.

There's a contest every month!

Go to www.1001DarkNights.com to subscribe.

**As a bonus, all subscribers can download
FIVE FREE exclusive books!**

Discover 1001 Dark Nights Collection Six

Go to www.1001DarkNights.com for more information.

DRAGON CLAIMED by Donna Grant
A Dark Kings Novella

ASHES TO INK by Carrie Ann Ryan
A Montgomery Ink: Colorado Springs Novella

ENSNARED by Elisabeth Naughton
An Eternal Guardians Novella

EVERMORE by Corinne Michaels
A Salvation Series Novella

VENGEANCE by Rebecca Zanetti
A Dark Protectors/Rebels Novella

ELI'S TRIUMPH by Joanna Wylde
A Reapers MC Novella

CIPHER by Larissa Ione
A Demonica Underworld Novella

RESCUING MACIE by Susan Stoker
A Delta Force Heroes Novella

ENCHANTED by Lexi Blake
A Masters and Mercenaries Novella

TAKE THE BRIDE by Carly Phillips
A Knight Brothers Novella

INDULGE ME by J. Kenner
A Stark Ever After Novella

THE KING by Jennifer L. Armentrout
A Wicked Novella

QUIET MAN by Kristen Ashley
A Dream Man Novella

ABANDON by Rachel Van Dyken
A Seaside Pictures Novella

THE OPEN DOOR by Laurelin Paige
A Found Duet Novella

CLOSER by Kylie Scott
A Stage Dive Novella

SOMETHING JUST LIKE THIS by Jennifer Probst
A Stay Novella

BLOOD NIGHT by Heather Graham
A Krewe of Hunters Novella

TWIST OF FATE by Jill Shalvis
A Heartbreaker Bay Novella

MORE THAN PLEASURE YOU by Shayla Black
A More Than Words Novella

WONDER WITH ME by Kristen Proby
A With Me In Seattle Novella

THE DARKEST ASSASSIN by Gena Showalter
A Lords of the Underworld Novella

Also from 1001 Dark Nights:
DAMIEN by J. Kenner

Discover More J. Kenner

Damien: A Stark Novel

From New York Times and USA Today bestselling author J. Kenner comes a new story in her Stark series...

I am Damien Stark. From the outside, I have a perfect life. A billionaire with a beautiful family. But if you could see inside my head, you'd know I'm as f-ed up as a person can be. Now more than ever.

I'm driven, relentless, and successful, but all of that means nothing without my wife and daughters. They're my entire world, and I failed them. Now I can barely look at them without drowning in an abyss of self-recrimination.

Only one thing keeps me sane—losing myself in my wife's silken caresses where I can pour all my pain into the one thing I know I can give her. Pleasure.

But the threats against my family are real, and I won't let anything happen to them ever again. I'll do whatever it takes to keep them safe—pay any price, embrace any darkness. They are mine.

I am Damien Stark. Do you want to see inside my head? Careful what you wish for.

* * * *

Hold Me: A Stark Ever After Novella

My life with Damien has never been fuller. Every day is a miracle, and every night I lose myself in the oasis of his arms.

But there are new challenges, too. Our families. Our careers. And new responsibilities that test us with unrelenting, unexpected trials.

I know we will survive—we have to. Because I cannot live without Damien by my side. But sometimes the darkness seems overwhelming, and I am terrified that the day will come when Damien cannot bring the light. And I will have to find the strength inside myself to find my way back into his arms.

* * * *

Justify Me: A Stark International/Masters and Mercenaries Novella

McKay-Taggart operative Riley Blade has no intention of returning to Los Angeles after his brief stint as a consultant on mega-star Lyle Tarpin's latest action flick. Not even for Natasha Black, Tarpin's sexy personal assistant who'd gotten under his skin. Why would he, when Tasha made it absolutely clear that—attraction or not—she wasn't interested in a fling, much less a relationship.

But when Riley learns that someone is stalking her, he races to her side. Determined to not only protect her, but to convince her that—no matter what has hurt her in the past—he's not only going to fight for her, he's going to win her heart. Forever.

* * * *

Tame Me: A Stark International Novella

Aspiring actress Jamie Archer is on the run. From herself. From her wild child ways. From the screwed up life that she left behind in Los Angeles. And, most of all, from Ryan Hunter—the first man who has the potential to break through her defenses to see the dark fears and secrets she hides.

Stark International Security Chief Ryan Hunter knows only one thing for sure—he wants Jamie. Wants to hold her, make love to her, possess her, and claim her. Wants to do whatever it takes to make her his.

But after one night of bliss, Jamie bolts. And now it's up to Ryan to not only bring her back, but to convince her that she's running away from the best thing that ever happened to her-- him.

* * * *

Tempt Me: A Stark International Novella

Sometimes passion has a price...

When sexy Stark Security Chief Ryan Hunter whisks his girlfriend Jamie Archer away for a passionate, romance-filled weekend so he can finally pop the question, he's certain that the answer will be an enthusiastic yes. So when Jamie tries to avoid the conversation, hiding her fears of commitment and change under a blanket of wild sensuality and decadent playtime in bed, Ryan is more determined than ever to convince Jamie that they belong together.

Knowing there's no halfway with this woman, Ryan gives her an ultimatum – marry him or walk away. Now Jamie is forced to face her deepest insecurities or risk destroying the best thing in her life. And it will take all of her strength, and all of Ryan's love, to keep her right where she belongs…

* * * *

Caress of Darkness: A Dark Pleasures Novella

From the first moment I saw him, I knew that Rainer Engel was like no other man. Dangerously sexy and darkly mysterious, he both enticed me and terrified me.

I wanted to run—to fight against the heat that was building between us—but there was nowhere to go. I needed his help as much as I needed his touch. And so help me, I knew that I would do anything he asked in order to have both.

But even as our passion burned hot, the secrets in Raine's past reached out to destroy us … and we would both have to make the greatest sacrifice to find a love that would last forever.

Don't miss the next novellas in the Dark Pleasures series!

Find Me in Darkness, Find Me in Pleasure, Find Me in Passion, Caress of Pleasure…

* * * *

Storm, Texas.

Where passion runs hot, desire runs deep, and secrets have the power to destroy…

Nestled among rolling hills and painted with vibrant wildflowers, the bucolic town of Storm, Texas, seems like nothing short of perfection.

But there are secrets beneath the facade. Dark secrets. Powerful secrets. The kind that can destroy lives and tear families apart. The kind that can cut through a town like a tempest, leaving jealousy and destruction in its wake, along with shattered hopes and broken dreams. All it takes is one little thing to shatter that polish.

Rising Storm is a series conceived by Julie Kenner and Dee Davis to read like an on-going drama. Set in a small Texas town, Rising Storm is full of scandal, deceit, romance, passion, and secrets. Lots of secrets.

About J. Kenner

J. Kenner (aka Julie Kenner) is the *New York Times, USA Today, Publishers Weekly, Wall Street Journal* and #1 International bestselling author of over one-hundred novels, novellas and short stories in a variety of genres.

JK has been praised by *Publishers Weekly* as an author with a "flair for dialogue and eccentric characterizations" and by *RT Bookclub* for having "cornered the market on sinfully attractive, dominant antiheroes and the women who swoon for them." A six-time finalist for Romance Writers of America's prestigious RITA award, JK took home the first RITA trophy awarded in the category of erotic romance in 2014 for her novel, *Claim Me* (book 2 of her Stark Saga) and in 2018 for her novel Wicked Dirty.

In her previous career as an attorney, JK worked as a lawyer in Southern California and Texas. She currently lives in Central Texas, with her husband, two daughters, and two rather spastic cats.

Visit JK online at www.jkenner.com
Subscribe to JK's Newsletter
Text JKenner to 21000 to subscribe to JK's text alerts

Discover 1001 Dark Nights

Go to www.1001DarkNights.com for more information.

COLLECTION THREE
HIDDEN INK by Carrie Ann Ryan
BLOOD ON THE BAYOU by Heather Graham
SEARCHING FOR MINE by Jennifer Probst
DANCE OF DESIRE by Christopher Rice
ROUGH RHYTHM by Tessa Bailey
DEVOTED by Lexi Blake
Z by Larissa Ione
FALLING UNDER YOU by Laurelin Paige
EASY FOR KEEPS by Kristen Proby
UNCHAINED by Elisabeth Naughton
HARD TO SERVE by Laura Kaye
DRAGON FEVER by Donna Grant
KAYDEN/SIMON by Alexandra Ivy/Laura Wright
STRUNG UP by Lorelei James
MIDNIGHT UNTAMED by Lara Adrian
TRICKED by Rebecca Zanetti
DIRTY WICKED by Shayla Black
THE ONLY ONE by Lauren Blakely
SWEET SURRENDER by Liliana Hart

COLLECTION FOUR
ROCK CHICK REAWAKENING by Kristen Ashley
ADORING INK by Carrie Ann Ryan
SWEET RIVALRY by K. Bromberg
SHADE'S LADY by Joanna Wylde
RAZR by Larissa Ione
ARRANGED by Lexi Blake
TANGLED by Rebecca Zanetti
HOLD ME by J. Kenner
SOMEHOW, SOME WAY by Jennifer Probst
TOO CLOSE TO CALL by Tessa Bailey
HUNTED by Elisabeth Naughton
EYES ON YOU by Laura Kaye
BLADE by Alexandra Ivy/Laura Wright
DRAGON BURN by Donna Grant
TRIPPED OUT by Lorelei James

STUD FINDER by Lauren Blakely
MIDNIGHT UNLEASHED by Lara Adrian
HALLOW BE THE HAUNT by Heather Graham
DIRTY FILTHY FIX by Laurelin Paige
THE BED MATE by Kendall Ryan
NIGHT GAMES by CD Reiss
NO RESERVATIONS by Kristen Proby
DAWN OF SURRENDER by Liliana Hart

COLLECTION FIVE
BLAZE ERUPTING by Rebecca Zanetti
ROUGH RIDE by Kristen Ashley
HAWKYN by Larissa Ione
RIDE DIRTY by Laura Kaye
ROME'S CHANCE by Joanna Wylde
THE MARRIAGE ARRANGEMENT by Jennifer Probst
SURRENDER by Elisabeth Naughton
INKED NIGHTS by Carrie Ann Ryan
ENVY by Rachel Van Dyken
PROTECTED by Lexi Blake
THE PRINCE by Jennifer L. Armentrout
PLEASE ME by J. Kenner
WOUND TIGHT by Lorelei James
STRONG by Kylie Scott
DRAGON NIGHT by Donna Grant
TEMPTING BROOKE by Kristen Proby
HAUNTED BE THE HOLIDAYS by Heather Graham
CONTROL by K. Bromberg
HUNKY HEARTBREAKER by Kendall Ryan
THE DARKEST CAPTIVE by Gena Showalter

Also from 1001 Dark Nights:

TAME ME by J. Kenner
THE SURRENDER GATE By Christopher Rice
SERVICING THE TARGET By Cherise Sinclair
TEMPT ME by J. Kenner

On behalf of 1001 Dark Nights,

Liz Berry and M.J. Rose would like to thank ~

Steve Berry
Doug Scofield
Kim Guidroz
Jillian Stein
InkSlinger PR
Dan Slater
Asha Hossain
Chris Graham
Kasi Alexander
Jessica Johns
Dylan Stockton
Richard Blake
and Simon Lipskar